the quiet
goings on

A COLLECTION

the quiet goings on

POEMS. STORIES.

Chris DiCroce

Tin Finch

For those we've lost.

Introduction

I have been trying to get to Baja for almost twenty years. The first time I thought about traveling to the mysterious peninsula was shortly after the events of September 11, 2001. In an effort to cope with that horrific event, I immersed myself in music and literature. With music, I gravitated to the songwriters, those with the ability to rearrange the pieces of difficult events in a way that I could understand and process. My go-to voices; Springsteen, Prine, and Petty.

I did the same with my reading choices. I sought solace in the stories about the wanderers and the survivors. Stories grown from the dirt of hardship and pain; with a sliver of triumph, even if it was well-hidden and required some digging.

One of my favorites was John Steinbeck. Through his stories, I found that I could deconstruct the American condition, examine the strata of human nature, and maybe make some sense of my own feelings and reactions. I reread *The Wayward Bus*, *Tortilla Flats*, and *East of Eden*. Then I dove deep into *The Log of the Sea of Cortez*, a book Steinbeck wrote with his friend, Ed Ricketts, about the magical waters surrounding a mystical peninsula called Baja. I stumbled upon it by accident. It was an accident that sparked an immediate love affair with a place I wouldn't get to see with my own eyes until this year.

Now – here I sit – in a small, dusty Baja town, six hundred miles south of the closed U.S. border as a global pandemic holds the entire planet hostage. China has ceased its production of the world's trash, airlines have stopped flying, the stock market is in freefall, and millions and millions of people are under stay-at-home orders in an effort to slow the spread of the coronavirus. The entire world, reluctant participants in the Great Pause of 2020.

As of this writing, I have yet to make any sense of it. But, I am hopeful that as the world views this event through a lens on the other side, it will realize that some good has come from it.

With regard to this collection, I don't believe there is any great importance in telling you the long version of how we find ourselves in Baja. It just happened, as things usually do with us. Basically, one morning we decided it would be a good idea to spend 23 days driving our 19-year-old Honda across the country, visiting friends and family, camping, and then ultimately crossing the border to an imaginary place that I had been building up for 20 years.

And somehow, it worked. But once we arrived, it was time to get to work. Having scrapped my second novel, I was at a bit of a loss as to how to begin it again and began to wonder if what I'd spent six months writing was pure shit and worth beginning again at all. Rather than sit and ruminate for too long (a perilous endeavor for someone like me), I gave myself a challenge. One that would keep me busy writing every day while I pondered over my previous book's future.
 The challenge? Write one short story per week for the duration of time that we were in Baja.

Here's how I envisioned it to work: Monday – come up with an idea. Tuesday – research it. Outline it. Wednesday – begin writing. Thursday, finish it. And by 5pm on Friday – have a completed second draft.

I was not to judge the quality of the idea nor was I to spend countless hours massaging or critiquing it, as I'm wont to do. The goal was to finish what I started. That's it.

The end result is twenty weeks' worth of words in their raw, honest form. For the most part, I've kept myself from obsessing and endlessly analyzing or rewriting.

I will say, once the news of this virus hit and I began to think about the safety of my family and friends, I found myself fixated on the events of the day with very little creative energy or focus left for the words.

Each day, as the news seemed to get worse, I went deeper down the rabbit hole. The long form suffered and shorter bursts in the form of poems began to emerge. Honestly, I was simply writing down whatever would come, and grateful for it.

I've chosen to include all of this in the order in which they were written, a period of time that began just before Thanksgiving 2019. As it stands now, we're starring down the barrel of July 2020 and there's no telling when it will end.

It's difficult to find the right words during these times. Words that I won't look back on years from now and view as manufactured or overly dramatic. And I don't know what things look like ahead of us. At the time of this writing, the United States is engaged in a battle for its soul.

What I do know is that years from now, my time in Baja will be as significant as it had always set itself up to be. This magical place inspired me to create something I'm immensely proud of.

And here it is, *The Quiet Goings On*. My own

collection of stories, written for the wanderers and the survivors. Stories grown from the dirt of hardship and pain with slivers of triumph and humor for those who don't mind a little digging.

c.

Table of Contents

There is a little voice in my head, indeed.
It comforts me in times of need.
And it simply says, keep going.

less words

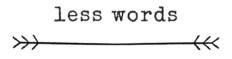

Happiness, That's What

This is the year that everything changes. It has to.
It simply can't go on the way it has been.
I'm going to believe in magic again – yours and mine.
And with all my broken pieces, build a castle.
But I should tell you – I'm getting off this train.
I'm sorry if we lose touch.
It doesn't mean I love you any less.
It just means I'm tired.
I've seen this all before – and before that.
I can see it up ahead, coming – again.
Not this time, amigo. Vaya con dios.

I'll walk – on my own with my own thoughts –
the good ones.
The others can go on ahead with you – lost luggage.
If it rains, I'll wait it out.
If I get hungry, I'll eat. Grow tired – rest.
When there are questions, I will seek answers,
truthful ones.
That's how this works now.
There's no more time for doubt
or counterfeit hope, opaque faith, or unfounded fear.
There's nothing but fierce with the time I have left.
Do the work. Stop lying about who I am –
to myself and to you.

I'm going to believe in magic again.
What's the worst that could happen?

laNG-gwij

Sound
Discovers
Connection
a way in –

Comfort

Inclusion
Disclosure
Confusion
Conflict

exclusion

Awareness
Resolution
No sound
Affirmation
Love

a way out

goodbye

A Walk in the City

Tall cranes attempt to fly.
Sidewalks wheeze metallic breaths.
We machine ourselves from place to place;
make our beds for better days.

The hearts and bones, they need repair
perhaps a walk beneath the moon's request;
some blood for nothing, but the price was fair
for a street fight that never was.

Just a man – spilling himself out on the night air,
shadow boxing, swinging wide.
A bit maudlin.
Let's move along –

there's nothing to see.

The Mission

Three hundred years –
that's a long time
to withstand the elements.
That's the mission.
No matter the weather
it is refuge.
However high the tide,
a dry place to stand.
The rocks and arrows remember
the mortars, a harquebus defense.
From a lectern to the arid dirt.
No, there's no water here but –
Jesús en Ti confío

We'll build a tower for the bells.
Bells to brush the sky,
ring elated tones
so full of worth that everything beneath
is just that – beneath.
With great height, adulation.
To topple would tell us what we already know –
that a bell is worthless as a breadbasket in the desert
on the ground with the rest of us.

These stone walls won't follow
a bell tower gone to sea.
Especially the bottom of a sea;
not in protest, but to flee – for a moment.
To snag a fisherman's net.

To feel – Nature in the ocean's kiss,
escape, silently – cradled for a spell
in soft silt.

To bring the hawk's song to the whales,
report back to the dirt and the lantern.
Now that they know, the bells can tell us all
the understanding – of the stars, the sun, and moon;
ring the wisdom of the waves.
Sing to us the songs of whales,
the mountains lament –
that they're missing the elevation
as grains of sand, the ocean's floor.
Different, like all of us, weathered.
The bells are telling –

But, we are not listening.
We've outrun their knowledge.
Time has marched on.
The songs of the hawk
don't interest the whales anymore
and, the songs of the whales matter less now
than ever to the dirt and the lantern.
They have no use for the wisdom of waves
or the understanding of the stars, the sun, and moon.
They have ambition.

The dirt wishes to conquer the mountain range.
The lantern seeks to outshine the sun.
And we've lost the ability to be amazed
at the ordinary within the extraordinary,
to marvel at the single stone within the wall.

The wall that makes up the mission
that provides refuge and a dry place to stand.
    Because the tide is rising
and the songs of whales are fading.
And the hawks have taken flight.

Specs

Today's my birthday.
Adulthood, I guess.
I had to get glasses.
Now, I see my youth differently –
Blurry.
That's why I had to get glasses.

war has no peace

At some point, the fight
becomes only with ourselves.
and war has no peace.
But – should peace come,
man will need a cause
and – being men,
the cause will be war.

Pinky Swear

We'll walk there,
together – and wander.
Then, I'll wonder
if you'll catch me
when what will be – is.
Know this.
I will catch you
when things change.

Different Now

It's spreading.
The machines have shut down.
We've locked ourselves in and things –
    appear dark.
Life interrupted, routines on hold.

Wash away – the sickness, the worry.
But it comes back, the worry.
This is not my problem.
It's not yours.
It's ours. All of us.

Buzzing, like flies at a screen door,
wondering what comes next.
How do we go on?
Will there be enough?
Nature is cleaning up our mess.

We're being shown what we can live without.
We're being reminded –
kindness survives disaster.
We're learning that some things will never make sense.
Parts of our old lives are gone for good.

Maybe that's okay.
And maybe, on the rush back
to what they called *normal*
we pause for a moment and decide
if it's worth the rush.

Eve's Shoulders

In she came – I noticed.
A sugar cube on my tongue;
Rounding her edges.
Dissolved into the room,
Quickly gone –
But, I remember.
A warm whiff
and the slightest hint of vanilla.

Today

Today is not yesterday
or the day before that.
Today isn't tomorrow
or any day after.
Today is a silver stallion
to be ridden only once
because tomorrow
today will be gone.

Rivers

Before you say, I just want to go back
to the way things were – realize
that there is no going back.
There is no normal.

There is only *before this*.

Where we were brought us to where we are –
and from here, there is only forward.
Life and time and rivers don't flow
in reverse.

Ducks

He waited until the very end to tell me he liked ducks.
We spent life speaking only of the nuts and bolts.
Never much talking, but a lot of speaking.
It wasn't for a lack of trying or – maybe it was.
Nor was it a lack of understanding; or maybe –

I tried again, remember the reach for connection.
On his eightieth birthday I asked what he'd learned;
to impart upon me the wisdom he'd been holding.
He blinked his eyes, working something over. I waited.
Don't take any chances – is what he said.

He's gone now and I recreate things –
so that they make sense, but they rarely do.
I simply move zig-zag down old roads;
and wonder (sometimes) why I'd never want to be a kid
again – if given the chance.
And I don't blame anyone – him or me.

Each of us played the card we were dealt.
But I know now – about the lack of understanding.
I never knew of his fondness for ducks –
and he could never grasp that my entire life
has been constructed from chance.

I'm Trying My Best

I'm trying my best to live in a world
with atom bombs and plastic body parts.
In a world where ancient empires crumble,
disappear like morning fog.
In a world where I feel connected
through the utter disconnectedness
that everyone seems to feel.
Where we fight for children that aren't yet here
but refuse to protect the ones that are.
A world that looks to the gods for answers
then ignores the answer.

Where the oceans are dying and nobody cares
that the dogs of war are the only creatures being fed
and the lessons of our past are being roasted
like marshmallows over the flames of our Republic.
Where it's impossible to run from anything anymore.
I want to – to fight for the world I knew before,
but everyone just stands there staring,
afraid to make a move. Waiting. For God.
And I'm left swinging at ghosts, knowing
that those who choose to do battle with ghosts
would do well to make certain and not become one.

I'm trying my best to live in a world
where the color of you don't matter
and a cupful of love gets me through.
With easier footsteps and less critical eyes
for those with stories I know nothing about

and whose battles I can't even fathom
because – everyone is swinging at ghosts.
And trying their best to live in a world
With atom bombs and plastic body parts.

more words

Bravo

J ack skidded the Jeep to a stop, barely missing the ragged pup. The dust cloud he'd been outrunning for most of the morning caught up. In the midday heat, after hours of speeding along molten tarmac, the clattering V8 announced a valve tap, a reminder to Jack that things needed attention.

Clapping the dirt from each thigh, he motioned to the driver of a tractor-trailer. More dirt – fine, like sifted flour – this time punctuated with the smell of livestock. Chinampo, packed ass to nose in a slow parade of fear and defecation. A wide, panicked eye stared him in the face as it passed. Jack imagined any chance at a stay of execution had also passed. "Lo siento, amigo."

On the far side of the road, Puro Burro jutted from

an earthen berm. The windowless, two-sided taqueria leaned like drunks atop a trash heap. Rough mesquite logs lashed together with hemp ropes and galvanized pipe straps formed a quartet of unsteady legs onto which the primitive roof was fastened. The long shadows of La Giganta were hardly sufficient for preventing the corrugated tin from reshaping itself in the desert sun. The place was empty save for two weather-worn vaqueros devouring the last of their chilaquiles and coffee. Jack picked the table farthest away. The plastic chair contorted under his weight.

"Hola amigo!" The voice came from behind a chest-high counter, through an oaky curtain of smoke, rich with the stench of dead animals. The sweating man never looked up, his shoulders excited with the movements of a jazz dancer, his hands slashing and scraping; metal on metal.

"Solo tenemos carne," he said.

Jack nodded, "Está bien."

A hirsute woman with fleshy arms swung a hand towel nearby, scattering hot ashes and flies. Her unaged, coffee-colored face glistened at its round edges. Her stout frame serpentined tables with an underwater grace that defied her rugged cultivation and disguised an unexpectedly delicate voice. "Somting to drink?" she said.

Jack bristled when she spoke to him in English. "Si. ¿Tiene cerveza? Pacifico?"

"¡Claro que sí!" said the woman.

Seconds later, she delivered a dripping brown bottle and waited as he untwisted a paper napkin from the mouth of the bottle and took a long swig.

"¿Estás listo?" She said, repeating, "You are ready?"

"Si, dos tacos, por favor."

"¿Algo más?"

"No, gracias."

Out of the corner of his eye, Jack saw the shadow of his unexpected visitor well before seeing the shadow's creator. The small dog he narrowly missed squashing moments before made its way toward him with the cadence of a broken toy. A few steps, stop. A few steps further, before pressing its matted skeleton to the filthy linoleum, raising only the pea-sized, chocolate circles of his eyes to meet Jack's. His rat tail swept tiny triangles, scattering small pebbles like tiger's eyes, waiting for assurance that it was safe to move closer. Transfixed on Jack, the pup didn't see the sliding chair coming, broadside into its midsection. The chair's momentum catapulted the wailing dog, skidding, flailing, tumbling down the dirt berm. The pup darted with tucked tail to cower beneath the jagged mud treads of the Jeep.

Jack turned to face the two cowboys, unable to hide the disdain. *Brothers*, he thought. Dark-complected with matching salt and pepper mustaches and a significant separation in age. The older, a cactus of a man, gaunt and leathered. Deep creases like desert arroyos fractured his pitted face. A salt-stained cattleman's hat hid everything above a lawless brow and tobacco-stained eyes. A broad smirk identified him as the heartless bastard.

The younger one, a bulkier oke, wore upscale

threads for a local taco joint; a faded line ran the full length of his wrinkle-free, dungareed leg. His chapped, split hands nervously twisted a small piece of baling wire in the gaps between his dulled teeth. He diverted his eyes and scraped the edge of one boot against the other, dislodging an imaginary dung.

"Amigo! He is a street dog," the old one said, proud of his English. "En wan week – he will be dead." He twisted a boot heel and never unlocked his gaze from Jack's.

Jack held his stare in a firm grip while he pondered the overt act of aggression. A tightness raced through his face, untransmitted, save for the imperceptible twitch in his left eye. Brawling in the dirt with a couple of vaqueros over a street dog was exactly the kind of shit Jack was trying to avoid. It stood as a direct contradiction to the only rule he carried with him like gold bullion: *be invisible*. It's why he came to this place – a place so far from every other place.

At the very moment Jack decided to disregard his rule, a sudden gust of wind arrived. A cyclone of dirt and trash spun through the shack like vandals, skidding tables and chairs, releasing a small mob of napkins and paper plates in a ballet with the dirt. The men braced against the freakish blast. The brothers bent themselves, calloused hands keeping their hats from being carried off in the duster. Jack stood and turned his back to debris, landing him face to face with the tall one. For a brief second, he considered throwing a squared fist into his bony jaw. That's when the woman appeared – from the dust itself. Holding a plate at the end of her extended palms, she said, "¡Buen provecho!"

Jack reclaimed his seat. The brothers handed pesos to the man behind the grill, the tall one laughing over his shoulder as they walked toward a flatbed Chevy. Jack backed himself down to invisible civilian, if that were at all possible.

Before she allowed Jack to set the plate down, the woman worked to straighten the checkered cloth and wiped it clean. The smell of bleach cut strong and burned the back of his throat. She wiped down the salt and pepper shakers and napkin dispenser, then spun a nervous circle, returning with a wooden tray and several bowls, each one different: diced tomate, cebolla, aguacate, and pepino.

"Another beer, señor?" she asked. Jack nodded. He could finally appreciate the parchment-covered paper plate cradling two steaming tortillas de maíz, each adorned with a small mound of wet, fragrant beef. For Jack, works of art proportionate to the masterpieces of Picasso and Pollock. He scooped generous helpings from the small terracotta bowls. Another cold beer arrived. The woman swiped her towel, cursing the relentless swarm under her breath.

Across the road, the pup was hesitant to leave its position in the dirt behind the wheel. A dime-sized, bologna tongue curled and flicked with each short little breath. Tiny eyes squinted, and every so often, the pup raised his nose to sniff the air wafting from the Burro.

Jack chomped the first taco with a bit of remorse, remembering the white, fearful eye of his condemned friend in the passing trailer, mortified at his own contorted expression reflected in the chrome of the napkin holder. There was no elegant way to eat these things. Toppings ooze, juices squirt and run glorious rivers down the chin and hands. Truth be told, few things touch the boundaries of heaven like a roadside taco.

Locked once again on Jack, the pup rose tentatively and shook a small desert storm. It crept from behind the wheel and moved cautiously into the dirt lane. So little and new to the world, unfamiliar with its harshness, its instincts under-developed and clouded by starvation, the pup didn't see nor hear the speeding four-wheeler. Too far into the road for a retreat, he turned, sucked his bones into the pulverized dirt, and waited to be done in.

Jack saw the four-wheeler. He shot from his chair, upsetting the table, and made a mad dash toward the road, yelling, furiously waving. The kid-faced driver swerved – skidded up the berm, nearly flipping before sideswiping Jack and speeding off. The tall one leaned both shoulders into the hood of his truck, roared with laughter, and twisted his boot into the dirt once more. The pup scuttled itself back to the safety of the small divot behind the wheel.

There was a slight, but noticeable tremble to his hand when Jack gave the hundred peso note to the man behind the grill. With his welcome well worn, he didn't wait for change. On his way out, Jack bent a knee to gather up the spilled parchment, tortilla, and scattered pieces of beef. The woman came quickly with a bucket and mop. He attempted to help her collect the pieces of broken beer bottle, but she shooed him away with the flies.

At the rear bumper of the Jeep, Jack got down on all fours. The pup retreated. Jack broke off a bite-size chunk of meat and tossed it to bounce in the dust. The dog darted backward.

"It's okay, buddy. I ain't gonna hurt 'cha."

The two brothers remained in position against the truck. The old one, still laughing and heckling, flicking assassinated Marlboro remains into the street. Jack eyed him from under the Jeep and regretted deeply not bashing in his rutted face. The younger one watched with great but unspoken interest.

The absurdity of all this was not lost on Jack. He was anything but invisible. Despite this, he lowered himself further, to a position flat in the dirt where he pawed himself forward with his elbows until the rear axle pressed him between the shoulder blades. He tossed a second piece and then a third. Then he rested his chin on the back of his hands and waited.

A small crowd had begun to gather at the Burro. The cook sat scrunched up on the berm with an arm draped over each bent knee. Beer in one hand, cigarette clamped between the first two fingers of the other. The woman cocked a hairy elbow and wore a broad smirk that needed no translation.

The pup inched forward, latched onto the closest morsel, and pulled it in. Then the next one, its needle-point teeth doing their best to handle a piece too large and too tough. Finished but unsatisfied, the pup moved closer. Jack reached out as far as he could, holding a piece of greasy beef between his thumb and forefinger. The tips of his boots dug ruts. His back strained, the muscles in his abdomen began to burn.

He whispered, "Vamos, amigo. No risk, no reward." And the pup came within centimeters of Jack's outstretched fingers. His tiny mouth tugged the meat free. Again and again, the tiny pup accepted meat from Jack's fingertips, yet remained out of reach. Jack retracted his arm to shake the blood back into his numbing fingers and the pup reeled itself in, as if on a fine tether of silk, unknowingly following the source; close enough for Jack to snatch him with his free hand. Frightened, the pup wailed and squirmed at the ambush.

The younger brother yelled and raised his hands. The cook swiped the cigarette from his lips, blasting a pillar of smoke into the air; his clapping so vigorous the cigarette broke at the filter and singed the hairy woman with the mop. She landed several blows to the cook's back and made grand gestures of dissatisfaction. Under her breath, she said, "¡Todos están locos!"

Jack laid the pup on a balled-up flannel in the bed of the Jeep. Quick work with a pocket knife turned a plastic Coke bottle into a small water bowl. He threw a leg into the wide-open truck, fired it up, and dumped the clutch. The oversized tires chirped when they caught the tarmac.

As he drove, Jack mulled over the long history that ran through the land he was traveling; like veins through granite, it was a deep and non-removable history of honor and hospitality. It's what drew him to the place where desert mountains kiss an unspoiled sea. It's what prompted a gringo loco to lay in the dirt and rescue a street dog. He'd seen enough fearful eyes.

Craning the rearview to reflect the bed of the Jeep, he saw no fear; only a sleeping pup, pink belly, and dirty paws. *You need a name*, he thought. With the afternoon sun tucking itself away and the wind whipping through the open Jeep, Jack said to no one in particular, "Bravo, amigo. Bravo."

Good Christian

Well, ain't this sumpt'n. This is how it ends – here in the goddamn snow? he thought. The coarse whistle in his breath reminded him of the first time his heart tried to quit eight years before. The day he commemorated the second anniversary of her death in the back of a wailing ambulance, bleary, in and out of consciousness, a twenty-something paramedic compressing his chest.

***

"Er he is! Man-uh-dee-owuh!" Frank, a dozer of a man shouted, spilling his coffee. A few yards away, Joey and Little Pete whistled and hooted. "I can't believe you didn't cawl in!" said Frank. "Shitty day like dis. I woulda' cawl-din."

"I haven't missed a day in thirty-four years," said

Jimmy.

"Yeah, yeah," piped Joey. "Everybody kiss da' ring!" Gesturing with wide open arms to the rest of the carriers. In a shrill, childish voice, one that matched his cub scout anatomy, Little Pete shouted, "Gather 'round, peasants. St. Gerard is here!"

At this early hour, the main branch bustled. Postal employees sorted the day's deliveries. Some pushed overloaded bins toward hungry trucks. With the bay doors wide open, the dank breath of a northeast winter dumped in, dragging its chains from the loading dock to the break room where Jimmy filled his thermos for the last time, its sage powder coating chipped and dented from three decades of service.

Joey leaned his bloated physique into the door frame. "Why ain't you wearing your Eagles hat? C'mon Jimmy-man... what the hell they gonna do, fire you?"

On cold days, Jimmy preferred the fur-lined trooper cap over his battle-worn, kelly green tuque. The twin earmuffs kept the cold out and the noise at manageable levels. Except for Joey's noise.

"Aren't you supposed to be pulling your split?" said Jimmy. "No wonder you're always gettin' written up."

Joey laughed and flipped him off. "I'm gonna miss you Gerard – you fuck."

Jimmy sorted and organized his bins. He pulled his route and lined out his street sequence the way he'd always done it, and loaded his truck in the same way he had for thirty-four years: flats first, then trays, then bulk mail bundles, neatly wrapped with two rubber bands. Then he made the same right turn onto South 31st Street, which, on this morning, was thick with slush already the color of ash. A steady wet curtain of flakes turned the commute into a parade of glowing taillights, intermittent flashes of amber, and spasmodic blue cop lights responding to the inevitable smash-ups.

"Everybody's in a rush," he said with a foggy breath. The windshield wipers offered a fresh perspective with each pass. *How nice it would be,* he thought, *if things could be that easy.* Inching his way through the slow turn into Chestnut Street traffic, Jimmy flipped a quick wave to a shivering police officer vigorously motioning him around a wreck. Jimmy laughed at the striking similarities in posture between the officer and the mechanized waving Santa over his shoulder in the Ludlow Federal Credit Union window.

First stop: Chestnut Street Apartments. For Jimmy, it was a solid way to start the morning with off-street parking and an attendant to watch the truck. He could leave it running, heat on. Next came Albert Greenfield Elementary School, then Carlo's Bakery. After that, the Helium Comedy Club, Federal Donuts (where he snagged two double chocolate), followed by Nom Nom Ramen, The Warwick Hotel, and the Sunoco at 18th and Walnut.

Jimmy loved being a carrier at this time of year. Secretly, he loved it all the time, but especially at Christmas. People were nicer. Lamp posts adorned with tinsel and white lights sparkled, adding life to the grayest of days. Storefronts glistened, bells rang, and kitchens all over the city unleashed holiday aromas into tightly-packed neighborhoods. Pumpkin, turkey, sweet-pastries, espresso, and fresh-baked bread had absolute authority over the ordinarily noxious airspace. A suffocation just fine by Jimmy.

Seniority gave Jimmy first pick of the best routes; people often wondered why he never transferred outside the city to an easier, less stressful one. For Jimmy, there was no other route but this one, the one he started running in 1985. To him, it was the best route. Not the most glamorous, chock-full of apartment buildings, schools, pubs, donut shops, and failing dry cleaners; but it took him down some of the most iconic streets, past some of the city's most revered landmarks: The Mutter Museum, Rittenhouse Square, JFK Plaza, The Academy of Natural Science, and City Hall. One especially narrow side street contained a dwelling not listed on any historic registry. It held no reverence, nor was it highly regarded by anyone except Jimmy Gerard.

The small row house on Quince Street was as uninteresting as a washed dinner plate. No festive lights, no tinsel. From the street, in the heavy snowfall, it was a rather ghostly place in a seemingly underwater world. Jimmy's footsteps crunched in the wet snow. Under his arm, the electric blanket was boxed and wrapped to perfection, and punctuated with an oversized crimson bow; he midnight green and silver streamers fluttered when he trotted the slate steps.

An elderly lady pulled the door open before a second rap, leaving Jimmy knocking on dead air. Her face held an excitement of someone being shot through with electrical current.

"Jimmy! É cosi bello vederti!"

"It's good to see you too, Angelina." He stooped to hug her. Into her shawl, he mumbled, "Come stai?"

"I'm good," she said in a soft Italian voice. "Vabbé... out of the cold! I want to give you your present!"

Angelina's silver hair was drawn back into a taut, lemon-sized bun of fine-silk, causing the corners of her cinnamon eyes to tilt up ever so slightly. He felt the delicate bones in Angie's hand as she pulled him through the parlor, holding it as he would a porcelain butterfly, her nails natural and well attended to.

"Angie," he said, "every year I tell ya not to get me a present, and every year, you do."

She raised her finger to his lips. "Sta' zitto."

Angie handed Jimmy an ornate wooden box, inlaid with opalescent pieces. "Per te, Jimmy. Per te." He was afraid to open it.

"Angie," said Jimmy. "You can't be spendin' money like this!"

She drew her shawl tight around her shoulders and smiled with closed eyes. A tear escaped over her high cheekbone and disappeared down the side of her face. "It's for your retirement."

"I can't take this, Angie." He stood, staring down at the etched silver pocket watch.

"Please," she said. "It was Nicolo's. It survived the second war – I fear it will not survive my children."

"Angie..."

"I'm ninety-two years old, fer Christ's sake! Wha-do I want from time?" Her voice trailed at the end.

Jimmy diverted his eyes to the box on the couch. "I gotcha' sumpt'n too. It ain't much. You wanna open it?"

Angie struggled with the cumbersome package but refused help. She arranged it on a shaky, knee-high table supporting the most crooked little tree. Wearing one frayed silk ball, a crochet snowman, and a smattering of red, green, blue, and amber lights, the small tree added a modest amount of spirit to an otherwise heartbreaking room. Meeting Jimmy's glance with visible embarrassment, Angie said, "Can I wait 'til tomorrow?" I'd like to open it on Christmas."

Jimmy descended the slippery steps, his Christmas cheer cut to the quick, and any signs of earlier footprints all but covered. From the street, he glanced back. Next to Angie's door leaned a straw broom, misshapen and well worn. Forgetting both his age and waistline, he raced up two steps at a time. Jimmy cleared Angie's front porch and steps, along with the sidewalk, fifty feet on each side, with the hope that at any minute, a carload of family would arrive and Angelina would not be alone on Christmas. Waiting for the truck to warm, over the blasting defroster, Jimmy heard the soft chime on his phone.

Jimmy, come to the shop. I'm pulling you.
Joey will finish your route.

Phil's text sent a rush of blood to his face. Only one other time had Jimmy left the route early. His family had planned to meet friends down the shore. With the 4th of July falling on a Saturday, Mary Elizabeth would drive down the Friday before. Their girls would arrive after classes and Jimmy, that evening after work.

His back soaked through and pressed against the black vinyl. Tiny rivers trickled into the crack of his ass. The dog days had arrived and crackled like bacon on flatiron streets. Agitation levels in the city rose with the mercury. Jimmy weaved his way through lunchtime traffic; excited at the promise of a holiday weekend, he cranked the truck's radio. A local sports show announcer was warning holiday travelers about a wreck involving an overturned tractor-trailer at the Jersey side of the Walt Whitman Bridge.

"Of course!" Jimmy shouted at the radio. "It's gonna take me all friggin' night to get to the shore, now!" He texted Mary Elizabeth to alert her and advised her to take the back way. It was longer, with more traffic lights, but it circumvented the busy highways and dead-stopped exit ramps. A few minutes before one, Jimmy's phone rang from an unrecognizable number. Unless it was Mary Elizabeth or one of the girls, he never answered his phone on the job. Minutes later, it rang again. It was his boss, Phil. Jimmy mashed the flasher button on the dash and pulled into the Starbucks parking lot.

"Hey, Phil, what's up?" Jimmy said.

"Jimmy..." Phil's voice was dry and serious. "Where are you?"

"Starbucks, Market Street. You want something?"

"Buddy... there's been an accident. Come back to the shop – now."

Jimmy heard the word – *accident* – but his mind made no connection. He glanced at the radio. "The one on the bridge? Yeah... I just heard."

Phil cut in, "Jim – It's Mary... she's... it's bad. Get here, okay? Just get here."

In the moments after, Jimmy felt faint. Twenty years he and Phil had known each other. Baptisms, birthdays, graduations; not once had he ever called him Jim. The heat that Jimmy barely noticed earlier cooked him like a blast furnace. His heartbeat pounded high-up; he could feel it thrumming in the small bones of his ears. The back of his head boiled. He swerved the van, cut lanes, at times careening up onto the sidewalk scattering pedestrians. He sped down one-way streets, cursing out his window at slow bike couriers and delivery trucks that blocked the way through.

Phil met him outside, along with two uniformed officers, one of which informed Jimmy that his wife had been killed in the accident on the bridge. The tractor-trailer, traveling at a high rate of speed, flipped in the curve and landed on Mary Elizabeth's Honda. The two vehicles careened into a concrete barricade. It took first responders over an hour to cut through the twisted metal. Quaking nightmares haunted Jimmy. He was unable to shake from his mind thoughts of Mary Elizabeth's folded body bleeding, suffering in heat – dying.

***

For what seemed like hours, Jimmy watched tiny icebergs slide slowly down the windshield, twisting, melting into rivulets. In the distance, snowflakes the size of nickels parachuted to the ground and it was at that moment Jimmy let surface what he'd known for a very long time: he was ready to be done. He typed:

I gotta make a stop.

Jimmy tugged the trooper cap from his head, stomped the slush from his boots on the black mat; muted thuds reverberated through the empty church. At the center aisle, he knelt and tapped out the signs of the cross. The harlequin pattern of gray and white marble pulsed and pulled Jimmy forward, toward the altar. But he didn't dare walk that center aisle anymore, not since his wedding day.

Without any recollection of having moved through the physical space, Jimmy found himself at his usual spot in the cathedral. The small alcove housed a collection of blood-red votives, arranged in rows, each a step higher than the one in front. Freshly lit candles, boisterous with their flames, sent a ribbon of carbon to darken the feet of Christ on the cross. Others flickered, sucked their last breaths, drowning in their own light. He crammed a folded twenty into the metal offertory box. Lighting a candle away from all the others, he knelt in fresh dents of the well-worn hassock, clenched his eyes so tightly his entire face wrinkled, and in a soft voice, he prayed.

"Through the prayers of Mary, virgin, and mother, I place in your care those I come to remember, especially my sweet Mary Elizabeth. I miss you, baby. I think 'a you every day." He paused, cleared his throat. "The girls are good. Maria's gonna live at the house while I'm gone, get back on her feet. Keep look'n out fer' er, she needs you. Deb is – Deb. Never misses a beat." It was always about this time Jimmy ran out of words and steady breaths. He made the sign of the cross and said, "Shine your light into the darkness of this world, baby. We need it."

Jimmy gave a start when he turned to find Father O'Malley standing statue-like with his hands folded in front of him.

"Need it indeed," he said in a thick Irish brogue. "I didn't mean to give ya' a fright."

"How ya doin', father?"

"Ah, it's Christmas Eve. If I were any better, son... I'd be twins." His humor turned somber almost immediately. "Light'n a flame for Mary Elizabeth, are ya?" With a searching chin, he continued. "Hard ta believe she's been gone ten years. Hard ta believe."

Jimmy swiped his eyes with his sleeve, "Father, I wanna thank you for everything..."

Father O'Malley stopped him with a raised palm and a shake of his head, "I understand today's your last day? Retir'n!" He tapped Jimmy on the shoulder with a soft fist.

"Been a long time, father."

Father O'Malley took Jimmy by the elbow. The two men walked slowly. "Ya know son, I've been servin' this parish for fifty-eight years – outlived most of my friends. Watched little ones grow big. Then watched them make mistakes. Nearly bitten me tongue clean through to keep from shoutin' my opinions, tethered me own hands to keep from boxin' some ears." The men stepped lightly through the echoes of laughter and footsteps. Father continued, "I gave witness to a lot of pain and to some of the most magical moments of my life." Father O'Malley turned; the two men stood toe to toe. "But, I don't need to tell you about pain, ay?"

Jimmy's eyes welled up.

"James," Father O'Malley stared straight into Jimmy's face. "My heart may not survive sayin' a goodbye." Father O'Malley's eyes filled. "You paid yer dues, son... been a good Christian. You don't owe anybody nuthin'. Go and be happy. You gotta try – fer all of us." Father O'Malley laid a gentle hand on Jimmy's forehead, "And, may God put luck on ya."

Jimmy breathed heavy streams of fog inside the cold truck. Bracing against the flood of emotion and choking back most of the tears, he cranked the engine. The weight of the day was more than expected. Exhausted, he was thankful that Joey had agreed to finish his route.

The clang of the metal door announced Jimmy's arrival into the empty space. Phil and Joey emerged from the break room. "Jesus... what the hell took you so long?" said Joey, walking briskly, pulling on his thick jacket. "You act like yer retired er sumpt'n?"

"Roads were bad." Jimmy handed his keys to Joey. "I was almost done. There ain't much more to go."

Joey grabbed Jimmy in a bear hug. "Merry Christmas, Jimmy. I gotta go." He jerked his hood to hide his face and didn't look back.

Phil handed Jimmy a steaming mug, "So... how's it feel? You ready to go?"

"It feels good." Jimmy felt an obligation to smile. "I mean – thirty-four years is a long time to be someplace."

"Sure is buddy. It sure is." Handing Jimmy an envelope, Phil said, "Christmas bonus."

Then he handed Jimmy a small box. "This one's from me. Sorry 'bout the wrapping."

Jimmy lifted the lid on the unwrapped box. "Cufflinks? You got me – cufflinks? Thanks. I don't know when I'll wear 'em, but..."

"Exactly!" Phil said pointing with his lip-stained mug. "I don't want you to ever wear 'em. Ever. They're a reminder – never do anything that requires you to wear cufflinks." Jimmy laughed. Phil continued, "Find a beach... forget this shit-hole. Don't ever look back."

"Will do. I just gotta shovel the driveway. You know Maria – can't drive in the snow for nuthin'. She'll go right through the damn garage. Then... I'm outta here." Jimmy zoomed his hand through the air. Neither of them knew how to break the silence. Jimmy rattled the cufflinks against the inside of the box.

***

Slumped against the motorhome on a partially-shoveled driveway, Jimmy recalled, with absolute preciseness, every detail of the young paramedic's angelic face. How an ambrosial scent of red apples and bergamot mixed with her candy-sweet breath. So clear, he could reach up and touch her; the single swath of chestnut hair that escaped her tight ponytail as it gently swayed with each rhythmic thrust.

Jimmy removed the cufflinks from a side pocket. His trembling hand failed to keep hold, and the small box spilled at his feet. He felt his vision fade and Jimmy knew they'd be worn only once.

Scrambled Eggs

The blue chair was so ominous that Cass chose instead to sit on a futuristic red vinyl stool and study it from across the room. Softly rolling a few inches this way and that, she eyed the blue monster's thick padded braces, designed for the sole purpose of opening her up, positioning her hips low and forward, and her ankles above her heart.

Splayed wide open like that, she imagined the worst for her private space. She envisioned goggled, pocket-protected spectators ogling her pudenda; hot man breaths up her flue, peering over the paper gown to see the woman attached. Cass had to reel these thoughts in quickly as she felt an increased pounding of her heart and the rising of a full-fledged panic attack. She closed her eyes and meditated to calmer breaths by reprinting on her memory the warm California sun she'd left behind. Then she remembered the sign.

Sleep Over The Ocean!

Cass couldn't stop staring at the words etched in the concrete arch spanning the Crystal Pier Hotel entrance. Standing beneath it on a clear day, a person might fool themselves into believing they could see clear across the Pacific to Waikiki. Across the street, seated at a table outside Kono's café, the 28-year-old kinesiologist sipped black coffee with little interest in fooling herself for a single minute more.

In any other neighborhood, an azure blue Bentley GT taking the only available handicap spot would garner some attention. She thought it resembled a Honda Civic after too many collagen injections and questioned whether the true object of her contempt was the car at all. The man, mid-forties with just the right amount of muscles, emerged wearing charcoal Nike workout pants, a cream-colored cashmere pullover, and sunglasses worth what she paid in rent. He stepped up onto the curb and sat across from her, his back to the arch.

"Are you gonna take those off or do I have to have this entire conversation with your astronaut glasses?"

"Cass – *you* asked to meet. I don't have time for this shit. I told Paige I was going to the gym. You got fifteen minutes."

She attempted a tight-lipped smile, dropped her gaze, and gently tossed her head in the direction of the GT to brush the hair from her face. That's what she told herself. Mostly it was an effort to shake away the *how the hell did I end up here* dialogue that was ambushing the calculated discussion she hoped to have. It was a question she'd asked herself a hundred times, usually while running along the beach, which is where she met the man now seated within striking distance. "Okay, Andrew. Let's get this over with."

A waitress arrived with two menus. Before she could speak, Andrew said, "I'm not staying. Thank you." Cass's body shifted in her chair. The young waitress pirouetted, but not before Cass reached her with a tap on the elbow.

"Excuse me –" she said, more tersely than she'd intended. "I'm staying... and I'd like the French toast, no powdered sugar. I'd like the fruit cup instead of potatoes, and I'd love some more coffee, please." The tail end of her order drifted up as if she'd all-of-a-sudden become unsure.

"She thinks we're a couple... fighting," he said with a smirk as the young waitress darted off.

Cass's expression was dry and unmoving. She refused to let herself react. Even allowing the corners of her mouth to drift up into the slightest of smiles would give Andrew admittance to a roped-off place inside her and be an automatic forfeit.

"I've thought about it. And – I'll do the deal. I'll be your donor." She tripped over the words, the bile in her throat tasted of humiliation. "On my terms, though. You have no say, none." Andrew sat deep in the chair. He bent his upper body far back, out from under the shadow of the umbrella. Cass was staring up his nostrils when he nodded. "Good," she said in a raspy whisper. "Twenty-five thousand. That's what I want.

Twenty-five, plus clinic expenses. Gas, hotels, meals... salsa lessons if I want 'em. That's the deal."

If a person searched long enough and to the vast reaches of the planet, it might be possible to find someone who spoke with such a condescending tone as Andrew Garrison. "Where you gonna go – after?" he said.

"That's none of your business."

"What about your apartment? Do you need me to..."

"I'm breaking the lease. My stuff's in storage. And, I don't need you – you've done enough." She paused then asked, "Does Paige know?"

Looking a little like a moveable wax figure, Andrew snatched the key fob from the table, extended his arm, and pushed a button. The Bentley's engine rumbled. Andrew stood as Cass's glare followed his frame skyward.

"Paige wants a baby, Cass. That's what she knows." He dropped a fifty on the table and stepped off the curb. Opening the car door, he said, "No phone calls. No texts." Staring into his open sunroof, he continued, "Email me your bank information and I'll do the transfer today. You're an employee. It's business." He slammed the heavy door and, through a rolling-down window, finished with, "Got it, Cass?" Andrew snatched the swaying disabled placard from the mirror and screeched the tires when he sped off.

"I got it – asshole."

"I'm sorry?" said a confused waitress as she topped off Cass's coffee mug.

Embarrassed, Cass said, "Oh – God... I didn't mean that for you."

The young girl tossed a glance toward the speeding Bentley, then back to Cass. "I'm sorry," she said. "Fighting sucks."

"What? Oh, we're not a couple. He's a client," said Cass.

"Oh, right." The freckled girl parted her lips slightly as if to speak, then nodded and walked away.

***

Cross-legged on the floor, Cass emailed Andrew her bank information. She typed another to Shirley, her landlord, and like the email sent to Andrew, it was brief and emotionless; chunks of pertinent information explaining the *what* and not a single syllable delegated to the *why*. She was breaking her lease and forfeiting her deposit. In Cass's mind, a small price to pay for a less dirty-feeling slate.

Closing her laptop, she made one last scan of the empty apartment. Scuffed walls and tiny imprints in the carpet were all that remained. Illegible hieroglyphics that would soon disappear under a fresh coat of some neutral, non-agitating shade of white and a vigorous vacuum. She tossed the keys on the counter and closed the door behind her.

Cass revved the 370 up the ramp onto 8 East with the sun behind her. It was dangerous to carry such a full head of steam with water-filled eyes. Seventy. Eighty. Eighty-five; the engine orgasmic at that RPM, hovering inches above the road, expansion joints clicking by with the same cadence as a New York subway car. She relaxed her bare foot, let up on the skinny pedal. It was five hours to Tucson and twenty-five more to St. Pete. A lot can happen, she thought.

***

The door opened, to Cass's visible relief, as Dr. McDaniel would have no difficulty understanding the anxiety with moments and procedures such as this. She had a flue of her own and Cass assumed, at some point, must have felt an uneasy draft or two in a chair similar to the blue monster.

"Hi, Cass. I'm Karen," she said. "Nice to finally meet you in person, after all the emails." Dr. McDaniel carried a manila folder and directed Cass into the chair. Cass scooted back, reclining so far she had to press her chin to her chest for any eye contact. Dr. McDaniel set off into the usual sort of small talk undertaken by physicians headed for a more serious discussion. And after a few snippets about the weather and inquiries about her trip in, Dr. McDaniel began with a barrage of pointed questions.

"I assume you haven't started smoking since your last email? No alcohol? Getting enough rest?" Cass nodded while Dr. McDaniel scribbled notes and made small check marks in tiny boxes. "You've been doing the Lupron and Gonadotropin injections?" Cass nodded again. Flipping pages, Karen McDaniel said without looking up, "My brother can be a bit vague and evasive with information sometimes. You've been his trainer for some time, I'm sure you know this." Dr. McDaniel smiled at a pallid Cass and said, "It's really incredible and – selfless of you to help Paige like this. She and Andrew have been trying to get pregnant for so long."

Cass felt the immediate urge to vomit upon the realization that Dr. Karen McDaniel was the sibling of Andrew Garrison, the man she'd been riding like a dime-store pony for the last six months. He had indeed been both vague and evasive with his recommendation of a competent and discreet fertility expert. Cass had the sinking feeling that Dr. McDaniel had no earthly idea about the events that led her to sitting in that chair and decided not to make any further eye contact.

"Paige is a sweetheart. I'm happy to help," she said. For Cass, to speak another word meant caving into a sinkhole of honesty. She felt revealing to Dr. McDaniel that she accepted twenty-five grand in fallopian hush money to help her infertile sister-in-law get pregnant might cause some friction. Cass had to disconnect from the serious thoughts as her pulse began to race again.

Dr. McDaniel noticed her complexion shift. "Are you okay, Cass? You want to take a break before we start?"

"No. Let's go. I'm just... I'm just a little nervous."

Cass stared holes in the ceiling tiles. Dr. McDaniel's gentle gloved hands directed her ankles up and guided her knees to a suitable position on the pads. Cass folded her hands over her navel and closed her eyes, capturing the small tears before they could escape, staging a small riot seconds later when the thin metal probe entered. Dr. McDaniel tucked low behind the barricade formed by Cass's raised knees. Next to Cass stood a black and white monitor, pulsing with an ultrasound image. A crude representation, but clear enough for her to see the shank of stainless impaling her, an alien plucking the granulosa gems from her insides like fresh pears. She felt the pricks. They stung hot. Her stomach twitched and contracted. She choked on her tears.

Dr. McDaniel spoke without raising up, muted through her surgical mask. "Hang in there. Almost done."

***

Cass stepped lightly through the lobby and rode the elevator alone. Her crotch burned, the ache reminiscent of her soccer days at San Diego State where, during a heated match, she got kicked in her spot. A blunt force trauma that resulted in a yellow card for the midfielder from UCLA and kept Cass's thighs from touching for nearly a week.

The heavy door closed behind her with a beautiful thud. She walked to the window and briefly entertained herself by creating storylines for each of the boats bobbing on moorings below; the entire Vinoy Basin immersed in the peach hues of a late afternoon sunset. Cass emerged from the emotional wreckage of the day hungry. She lifted the receiver and perused the menu until a voice answered. "Yes, hello – can you send up a bottle of Veuve Clicquot, please? The grilled chicken... mixed veggies as well. A side salad would be great. Sure, strawberry vinaigrette is fine." Her voice was soft, barely above a whisper. "And – could you please just leave the cart inside the door? I'm not feeling very well. I'm going to soak in a tub. Yes, I'm sure. Thank you."

The faucet shot a furious thrust of scalding water. Loud and gushing, it steamed the mirror instantly. Cass lifted her shirt over her head and unclipped her bra. She unbuttoned her jeans. With a slow swerve of her hips, they slid to a warm heap around her ankles. She wiped a swath of clear mirror and stood studying her reflection. She noticed how different the two sides of her face appeared. One woman she recognized, and then another. She fixated, as she had many times before, on the unevenness of her breasts, the left a little lower and fuller than the right. Considering the events of the day, it no longer bothered her.

The Other Son

Sunny Meadows Nursing Home sat on a piece of property bordered on its north side by the high-speed rail. To the south, the newly-widened Blue Route, a main artery for all those who had the grave misfortune of working in downtown Philadelphia. Surrounded on all sides by a forbidding, chest-high stone wall, and in stark disagreement with their lovely brochures, it was neither sunny nor meadowy.

The only sections of mowable grass were horse trough-sized islands floating in a vast sea of meticulously lined parking spaces. Its mid-70s brick exterior, single-pane windows, and sagging gutters informed anyone who cared to notice everything they needed to know about how much nursing was actually occurring within its walls.

For a mere seven thousand dollars a month, residents at the Meadows were guaranteed only the finest mashed peas and purest of pure high-fructose corn syrup. They could rest easy behind top-of-the-line security doors without the slightest worry of being exposed to the harassment of dignity or human decency. It was the highest-quality neglect.

As the only car in the lot, Charlie wondered if the place was open. He pressed the rectangular doorbell and waited to be buzzed in. Behind the reception desk, a delicate woman wilted in a lopsided wheelchair, the rubber on one wheel all but gone. Charlie wanted to straighten her. She smiled at him through thick lenses with eyes the size of walnuts. He signed his name and walked the few steps to the elevator.

Tilting the registry, she said in a soapy voice, "You're the priest?"

"No."

"Mm," she said, disappointed. "You're here for the meatloaf then."

Charlie held an emotionless expression, waiting for the elevator door to close. Each time he rode that elevator, it seemed to Charlie that he lost a small piece of whatever soul remained in him. The second-floor temperature forced him to remove his coat. The long hallway looked like a two-lane road dotted with broken-down cars. On the right, a railed bed. In the center, a body curled up like a spaniel under too many blankets. A few feet further, on the opposite shoulder, a woman in a wheelchair spit in her hand and pressed her kneecaps hard into the wall. Further still, an unshaved black man shuffled a walker and dangling bag of fluid. Then a nurse, then a rack of misshapen food trays.

Charlie drifted through the odorous gauntlet of boiled beans, urine, and bleach. Leaning into the second-floor desk, he said to a large black woman in scrubs, "Afternoon – I'm here to see Carl Rhuda." Charlie waved a folded piece of paper.

"You the priest?"

"No... the other son. Where is he?"

"In his room," she said with stern, unblinking eyes. "This is the third time."

"Okay – I'm sorry. I had no idea he was..."

"There won't be a fourth. You understand that, don't you, Mr. Rhuda?"

Charlie nodded and walked away. He rapped twice and pushed on the heavy door. Carl Rhuda's long frame was fully extended on the unmade bed, legs crossed with one palm behind his head; dressed for a walk in the meadow wearing dungarees, t-shirt, buttoned flannel, shoes, and socks. At the end of his outstretched arm, gray fingers cradled a remote. His thumb changed channels with steady taps.

"Well, look who's here," Carl said, without looking at Charlie.

"Hey, pop."

"You bring me any soft pretzels?"

"No, came straight from the airport."

"Figures," Carl said. "They're kicking me out. Medicaid ain't payin' enough. A veteran – you believe dat? Bastards wanna throw me out on'a goddamn streets."

"They're not kicking you out because of your Medicaid. They're threatening to kick you out because you keep assaulting the nurses."

Carl dropped his arm and looked at Charlie. "Assault?" he said, waving his hand. "That's what they said... assault? Screw 'dem. I ain't assaulted nobody. Let 'em kick me out. I could give a shit. And I... I ain't goin' nowhere wit' you."

Charlie stepped closer to the bed and pulled the letter from under the folded jacket draped over his arms. "Dad, you can't grab the nurses' crotches. What the hell is wrong with you? Honking their breasts isn't funny. Nobody thinks you're funny."

Carl chuckled. "I ain't hurtin' nobody. I'm eighty-one years old. Who'my gonna hurt?" He twisted a corner of the blanket, "I'm a fuckin' veteran."

"What you are is lucky that they haven't called the cops."

"Cops? Psh... where's your brother? Why ain't he here?"

"I haven't talked to him – not in a couple years. Guess he's at the rectory."

"So – you flew in to save your old pop – Mr. Big Shot."

"I'm not doing this," Charlie said, touching his father's leg. "Going down the same road we go down every time I see you."

Carl flinched. "Every time? Please, you ain't been here in years."

"I don't think you wanna have that conversation again – who's been around and who hasn't," said Charlie. Walking to the foot of Carl's bed and directly into his eye line, Charlie continued. "I flew in because I got a letter that said you were sexually assaulting nurses, smoking in your room, and paying the kitchen staff to get you booze." Carl turned his face to the window. "This is it – your last last chance," Charlie said. "You understand that, right?"

"Who else got the letter?" said Carl, refusing to recognize Charlie.

"I don't know who got the letter."

"Pauly... Pauly should be here. Marian should'a – " Carl stopped mid-thought.

"Marian?" Charlie said. "The woman who put you here, sold your house, and moved to Largo? That Marian?" Charlie caught himself, knowing nothing good ever came from revisiting the old growth with Carl. Over the last decade, Charlie managed to cultivate a small patch of ground that he could stand on. It became his alone and he roped it off, preventing the history of others from contaminating the soil.

"I don't know if Pauly's at the same parish. He could be anywhere." Charlie returned to Carl's bedside. "To answer your question – they didn't come because they're probably tired of this shit." Charlie grabbed his father's bony leg. "I'm tired of this shit." Carl jerked his leg free.

"Then get the hell outta here. I don't need nothin' from you. I didn't ask you to save me."

"I'm not here to save you, pop."

Carl's lips parted. The muscles in his face went slack with a hint, if only for a brief second, of disbelief. Then, all at once, decades of rage and contempt corrugated Carl's face. He raised the remote and began to mash the buttons.

Fair Fight

Love. Is there anything, anywhere with as many sharp edges. It looks so cozy from here, outside. Everyone smiling, laughing; reminiscing in the warm light of Kathleen's kitchen. Crowded around the granite island, stuffing their faces with neatly-cut squares of meat and expensive, stinky cheese impaled with little harpoons to make it easy; clean.

All of them here to celebrate Sharon and me. Thirty-five years of wedded bliss, today. There is an absolutely certain and unforgivable banality that accompanies a celebration like this and I can only take so much before I retreat to the deck for an illegal smoke, and to enjoy my scotch without so much as a single tight grin in response to the asinine remarks about the length of time we've been together.

It's easy to get tangled in the wisteria of nostalgia on a night like this. Easy to flip back through the file folders, pull out and put back a host of memories that you can't remember ever living. Meeting before we were old enough to drink, then waiting until after college to make it official, telling ourselves we'd be older and wiser. Waking before dawn to make love the way new young lovers do, Sharon darting off to grad school, her tousled hair still damp with sweat. I pulled the sled, happy.

"You gonna stay out here all night?" Kathleen said. Apparently, I had drifted further into the ether of nostalgia than I thought.

"Is that an option?"

"Nope."

"I just needed some air. It's a lovely evening, Kat. You've outdone yourself."

"Thank you, daddy. But – everyone is asking where you are."

"Everyone?"

"What does that mean?"

I had no intention of actually saying that – *everyone*. It felt childish the minute it escaped my mouth. My mind was occupied, watching Sharon through the window, talking to my friend Richard. It's been going on for years. Neither of them is particularly adept at hiding it from me, although I'm not sure they care.

"I'm sorry. I was trying to be funny."

"I know you hate these things, but it's a big night. Can you please try to enjoy it, for mom?"

Kat raised herself onto the tips of her toes, wrapped her arms around my neck. She was firm and reassuring. Over her shoulder, Richard was touching my wife on the wrist, talking through a smile, holding a glass wrapped in a napkin with his free hand. Drinking my scotch, not leaving behind any prints. I wondered if he took the same approach when he fucked my wife.

"Wait a few minutes before you come in. You smell like pot." Kat straightened my collar and walked away, so grown up and beautiful, like her mom. I was glad she had Sharon's genes – most of 'em – and hopeful that the ones responsible for Sharon's breast cancer would remain dormant. I'm not a praying man – until it comes to a double mastectomy.

Funny, the things you remember in pivotal moments, the both of us hairless on the eve of her surgery. I was the imposter and everyone knew it; my eyebrows betrayed me. The months that followed were some of our darkest, with life's unfathomable cruelty on display as Kat battled the awkwardness of her growing teenage breasts in full view of a mother who'd just lost hers. For almost a full two years afterward, we didn't speak of anything much past survival. "No future talk," Sharon would say. The fruits of regular life, things like vacations, fell away like the leaves of a sugar maple. They were there, on the ground around us, but we didn't dare notice them. We simply clung to the bare branches of recovery and reconstruction. Then, one day, I forced the issue. I suggested we take a trip.

***

Seville's orange blossoms were in full regalia. They spilled their aroma all over us as we tripped through hidden squares in the ancient city. Sharon had regained much of her strength. Her appetite returned – for the spinach and chickpeas, and the pork whiskey and sangria, but never for me.

On the day before returning home, we sat for a last sangria in what had become our favorite bodega, adjacent to the hotel. When Sharon's body protested after a long day of walking, she retired to the room. I took mine by the window where the owner, Don Carlos, would join me on prior visits, gesturing and correcting my deficient Spanish. We drew a direct line through Hemingway's cafés, and I didn't mind that the connection was obvious, and one that could have been entirely fabricated on his part.

I enjoyed it – for the first time in a long time – a regular conversation. One that wasn't centered on cancer, emotional requirements and expectations, or end-of-life decisions. A conversation that didn't end with, *I don't expect you to understand how it feels*. No matter, I still felt guilty, for enjoying.

That day, Don Carlos invited us to watch the first paseíllo of the season. La Maestranza bullring was a few minutes' walk from the hotel, and the opening parade was one of the most spectacular in all of Spain. I had great difficulty with the barbarous event, but it wasn't for me to criticize my host's centuries-old customs. I thanked him for the invite and excused myself with, "I'll check with my wife." Climbing the terracotta steps, I considered not mentioning the invite at all. I knew Sharon deplored animal abuse and macho sporting events that, as she put it, were a bunch of guys measuring their dicks and hitting each other in the head.

Sharon was just out of the shower, her bare back dripping. She clenched the towel to her chest. Her expression in the fogged mirror was far away, dreamy. I was interrupting.

"Don Carlos invited us to watch the opening ceremonies for the bullfight today."

"What did you tell him?"

"I told him I'd ask you. I didn't think you'd want to go – bullfighting and all."

"I'll get dressed."

I was not fully in attendance watching the parade pass from the curb. I was, instead, observing my wife's changing expression as Don Carlos explained what each participant was responsible for and the nuances of matador seniority. I was also not in full understanding of how orchestrated the torture was. In my mind, a guy – in a ring – faced down a bull. He swung a cape and people cheered. After a sufficient amount of spectacle, the man killed the bull and people cheered some more. Watching the rows of elaborately dressed men march by, it became clear to me the performance was not so simple. More than a dozen – in suits of light, reflective threads of gold and silver – puffed their chests, proud in their ability to inflict a great and imminent suffering.

Without notice, Don Carlos grabbed Sharon and me by the hand and towed us into the river of people following the procession. He moved swiftly, almost at a jog. Sharon was trotting on the balls of her feet, giggling. I felt a sickness at the sudden realization that we were in for more than a parade. Unbeknownst to us, our attendance at the paseíllo was taken as an acceptance to the entire event. To refuse Don Carlos' generosity would be a grave insult. Still, I gently protested, slowed my pace, and pulled free from his grip. Sharon stopped giggling. Her lips parted and then shut tightly. I asked if we could speak for a minute, alone.

"Well, that was rude," she said, with her back to me.

"I told him I thought it was cruel – and it is," I said, catching my breath. "You used to feel the same. When did you develop this sudden interest in bullfighting?"

"Today," she snapped. "You wanted to come to Spain, and now – we're here."

"Me? Sharon, you've been talking about Seville since grad school. *That's* why we're here."

She repositioned the shawl to cover her shoulders. "He invited us. We should go."

We walked in single file behind Don Carlos. Vendors shouted. A cool breeze kept the passages of La Maestranza Arena chilly. It crackled with anticipation and the smell of frying pig skin. Don Carlos shouted over the crowd, "We are the oldest bullring in Spain." He continued, "The people of Seville, the most expert and unforgiving of all the world!" I drifted away at the word unforgiving. It slowed me like chain around my ankles.

We reached our spot. Concrete benches circled the ring. We were close to the fight. Too close. The moisture in my throat went away and it began to close, shut tight with rage. I spoke no words when Sharon asked me where I wanted to sit. Instead, I put Don Carlos between us. He was going on and on with endless details.

"La suerte de capote, the first stage," he said. Then, holding up a finger, he repeated himself. "El capote – how you say en Inglés... cape? Here, the toreador will measure the strength of the bull. The way he charge tell him many things."

I stopped listening again. Don Carlos leaned his head close to Sharon's and kept on. I watched thousands of unforgiving people fill the benches. A sweaty woman, quivering with excitement, leaned into me. My mind told me to *get up, walk out*. I didn't. I sat there and looked on as a dozen men, some on armored horses, prepared to outnumber a terrified animal.

The tactical brutality began as Don Carlos said it would, with a cape and ceremonious waving and gesturing. It was after the picadors, riding heavily armored horses, entered the ring that the bleeding came. They were there to taunt – provoke the bull into repeated attacks on the horse. With each charge, the picador stabbed into the bull's shoulders with long-handled pikes to reduce his strength. Each time he plunged the pike, a fountain of dark blood shot from the creature's back. The bull charged again and again, smashing the horse. Wide swaths marked the points of impact. Don Carlos voiced his appreciation. He clarified for me that such great art involved wounding the animal carefully, not too much or too little.

I stole momentary glimpses at the unfamiliar

woman seated next to him, the one who used to be my wife. I stared at the side of her face. Her smile was one of extreme satisfaction, on the verge of becoming an all-out grin, gratified to watch something else suffer for a change. It felt like the end of something. So much around me competed for my disgust.

I wanted to leave, but no one is permitted to leave or enter during the fight. I sat for a moment longer, contemplating the after-effects of my walking out. The bull swung a heavy tail. I imagined his thoughts. Thoughts I know I'd have.

Why me? I'm not a maneater – no threat to you. You unleashed an army to test me, torment me, tire me out; bleed me dry. I'm so severely damaged, it can't ever be a fair fight. But – if you miss or kill me imperfectly, you will be over.

Several men prodded him into position for the next stage. There were so many directors of his demise. I stretched my back to see the matador, the one labeled *most courageous.* He was waiting behind a large barricade while his subalternos stabbed the still-willing-to-fight bull with colorfully-decorated, barbed harpoons. They stuck deep and hung heavily.

Don Carlos said, "The bull is tired. The banderillas revive him. When the harpoons are driven in, the courage and bravery of the bull will anger him. He will want to charge and be proud again. It is beautiful and very much dangerous!" I didn't respond. He went on, "The intention is to weaken the muscle in the neck – to get the bull to drop his head."

I stood and pushed my way past the jeers. I was on my own. The matador emerged from his barricade as I climbed the stairs. The sudden eruption of noise startled me... and the bull. At the exit tunnel, I turned for a last look at his ridicule. Long streams of snot spilled from his nostrils; his eyes were wide and looking far off. A once majestic carriage sagged with pain. His black hide glistened in the late afternoon sun, soaked in a life pouring from inside. The day's aim had been achieved; his proud head hung low.

***

Funny, the things you remember in pivotal moments. I drained the last of my glass. The remnants of ice felt good against my nose. I watched Sharon through the window. We haven't spoken of bullfights and we've talked no further about cancer or my lack of understanding. I've arrived at a place. I know the surgery took things – and left behind me. And since then, it's been a beautiful and very much dangerous dance, meant to weaken the muscle, lower the head. Something else I know – the fight is rarely, if ever, about the bull.

A Gathering of Lawyers

Coal Foot is a shifty little man. He walks, not with the gait of an athlete, but rather, one that suggests he's pinching an apple between his knees. His arms swing haphazardly like a marionette, but only from the elbows down. I don't say this to slight the man. It's merely an observation, one of many I should make during a typical day.

You see, I don't get out much, and I can only listen to Phyllis postulate on the rotatory movements of the humans for so long before the awnings of my eyes begin to droop. Which is precisely why I was so magnificently captivated by the discussion Coal Foot and Iceman were having. Oh sure, they refer to themselves with fantastical names; their true titles are far less exceptional – Jeffery and Ed. There are others not in attendance at the moment. One with the handle of Thunder Conductor. Another calls himself Sky

Painter, and then there's Moonshine and O-Zone.

I would laugh – if I could. The energy these men consumed in coming up with such nonsense would go much further, I believe, if it were directed at, say, fixing the sidewalks in Barclay Square or resolving, once and for all, the traffic conundrum at the criss-crossing of Union and Mahoning Streets. Nevertheless, I returned to my eavesdropping.

Judging by the official-looking letter and Coal Foot's phraseology, I suspected their conversing involved a legal matter, some sort of litigation being levied against someone familiar. Iceman guffawed at first, and I felt as though my afternoon entertainment was over before it began. Then he rubbed his chubby, hirsute face and said, "You can't be serious!" and my heart lifted.

"It's from the District Attorney's office," said Coal Foot.

All at once, the moment took on a greater seriousness when the remaining members of the so-called Inner Circle arrived, being that it was middle of the afternoon when most citizens should be at a place of employment or, like me on a normal day, napping. With such an official gathering being called in the broad light of day, I began to wonder who'd been murdered.

Coal Foot briefed the group on the details as he knew them and passed the letter around. Several of the gentlemen immediately began pushing on small squares of glass and spoke with hushed voices into the same contraptions. Such behavior is frowned upon in the Gobbler's Knob Library, and having lived here for as long as I have, I suspected a reprimand was about to arrive. But no such event occurred.

Moonshine, reading the letter, said, "This is preposterous."

"Read it aloud," said Sky Painter.

Moonshine shook his head in disbelief, hands on his hips. I was also waiting, with a great eagerness, to hear of this preposterous news. Moonshine motioned for everyone to sit. Addressing the members from the north end of the leg desk, he cleared his throat and began to read.

"*It is the state of New York's position that Punxsutawney Phil willfully, with premeditation and intentional design, misled the people to believe the arrival of spring would come early. The groundhog residing at 300 Mahoning Street committed a felony against the peace and dignity of the people of New York.*' Jesus H. Christ – this is ridiculous!"

"Is that it?" asked O-Zone. "Is there anything more?"

Moonshine reluctantly continued. "*I hereby charge him with the misrepresentation of spring.*' That's it. It's signed, Erie County Prosecutor, K. Donn Plotkin, whoever the hell that is."

Moonshine was right, it was absolutely preposterous. I've never misrepresented anything in all my life. I've never been to the great state of New York, as far as I know.

"This is some sorta publicity stunt," said Coal Foot. "You remember that group of knuckleheads, the ones who sued us a while back?"

"That was the year the New York City mayor dropped Staten Island Chuck. Poor fella," said O-Zone.

"Poor fella? The mayor was an asshole."

"I was referring to Chuck. He died right there on the platform."

"All those kids, crying on the TV," Moonshine said. "Definitely not a good day for Groundhog Day."

"They claimed animal cruelty, wanted us to stop using the real McCoy," Coal Foot pshawed. "The old boy's as happy as a judge in a whorehouse. Besides, who in their right mind would ever travel to see an animatronic groundhog?" Coal Foot answered his own question. "No one, that's who."

"Gentlemen, I know how we can handle this," said Iceman.

"Tell them he's a groundhog?"

"Don't be silly O-Zone. We fight."

"Yes!" said Sky Painter. "Bastards!"

"Amen! It's what we do with such esteemed certificates!"

"I don't mean to challenge the gentleman from Vanderbilt," said Moonshine. "But couldn't we settle? There has to be something Mr. Plotkin is seeking. Maybe a call to his office is in order. I'm happy..."

Iceman interrupted, "With all due respect to the gentleman from Princeton, the great state of Pennsylvania is under siege. More specifically, our beloved municipality. Not to mention a pillar of our community's character has been assailed – Phil. I'd rather eat an entire Caesar salad in the men's room at Penn Station than settle with Mr. Plotkin."

From my den here in the library, I've been able to learn all sorts of things. Most leave me quite confused, as I rarely have the occasion or mental capacity to assemble the entire puzzle. I'm usually left gnawing on bits and pieces of conversations such as these, and, as my wife Phyllis will tell you, I'm quite competent when it comes to exaggerating the confections of my imagination. While I was honored these men would take up arms for me, it was my intention to dissuade them immediately. While it is true that I possess some amenities of the higher civilization, words are not among them. My vigorous scratching on the glass, I fear, was misinterpreted as marmot encouragement.

"Look..." Sky Painter exclaimed. "Phil agrees. He's waving us on."

"Gentlemen, let's take a vote. A show of hands for all those in favor of fighting this summons." Iceman was perplexed at O-Zone's nonparticipation, his hands folded in front of him on the table. "O-Zone, is there a problem?"

"Yes – yes, there is."

"Would you like to voice it to the gentlemen?"

"Sure. I think we should just tell the District Attorney – this Mr. Plotkin fella – that Phil's a damn groundhog. He eats kale, digs holes, and sleeps all goddamn day. He... he can't mislead people, Harvey. He's a goddamn groundhog."

"O-Zone, if we tell people that Phil's 'just' a groundhog, they'll stop coming to the Knob. The economic impact would be catastrophic. People travel thousands of miles in the dead of winter, stand in fields holding signs, and they come to see the seer of all seers, the hognosticator himself. If we tell them he's a groundhog, then they'll know he's just a groundhog."

The complexity of Iceman's argument was impeccably put, but lost on me. However, it didn't seem to fog the rest of the Inner Circle. The gentlemen rose from the table and gathered their hats and coats as gentlemen do when they prepare to leave someplace for another place. I must admit, I was a little winded from the intellectual exchange and felt a nap coming.

Coal Foot said, "Gentlemen, what say we reconvene at the Candleman for a proper dram? We can continue when our logic is better primed."

"Marvelous idea," said Thunder Conductor. "I should say, this is an easy fix for men like us; we should make quick work of dispensing this indictment. I mean – it's not as if we're trying to fix the sidewalks in Barclay Square."

Waterman

Mickey knew the autumn crabbing season would end early. Last year, it lasted until six days before Christmas. This year, the season closed the day before Thanksgiving. His best shot at a good year just ended.

Suspiciously warm, it was not what a November day looked like back before the bay started rising and towns began sinking. Missing were the low gray skies and brisk Chesapeake winds. In the pilothouse, something else was conspicuously absent – the triumphant, profanity-laced banter and offensive hand gestures that punctuated the end of a successful day. There was only a faint taste of carbon in the air and the steady churning of grinding twin diesels.

The RPM drop at red marker 8 was the crew's notice to ready the lines. T-Bone went to the bow in scuffed orange bibs and a black t-shirt. He bounced a tangled dock line with one hand and gulped a last swig from a Coors Light can. Cry Baby leaned heavily with two hands on the port gunwale at the stern. Mickey drifted Kim's Fable into the causeway, swung the bow up into a lenient breeze, and backed, stern in, easing the old deadrise to a stop between the pilings.

"November's a bitch, Mickey," said T-Bone, cleating off the aft spring line. "Nobody knows anymore when they'll run south. Weather's so fucked – sixty degrees at Thanksgiving?"

Mickey cut the engines and flipped switches on the instrument panel. The gulls grunted and squawked overhead. T-Bone underhanded a carcass high in the air, fully entertained by the aerial battles that ensued over a dead crab. Cry Baby lit a fresh Marlboro in between the shuffling of full bushels onto the dock. His face was tight, holding back bad news that needed to be delivered.

Mickey felt something should be said, to no one in particular and to everyone. "I thought for sure they'd be running 'tween Bloodsworth and Smith. Maybe we should'a gone further north, to Hooper's. Who knows. There's no use second-guessing – season's done."

Cry Baby's teeth bit hard into the filter. A ferocious, exhaust-colored handlebar streaked with strands of silver hid both lips and ran to his jawline. "Yep, it's done, alright," he said. "I'll run these bushels to Handy's. You wanna give 'em a call, tell him I'm on the way so he don't close?"

"Thanks, Cry," said Mickey. "I'll see you at Grifters?"

"Naw – I'm gonna pass, Mick. Kelly'd crush my balls she finds me sittin' at the bar – season we had'n all."

"Alright. I'll see ya tomorrow then – Kim's gonna lay that bird on the table at three o'clock sharp. Come by whenever."

Cry stared off at nothing specific. Mickey and T-Bone watched him take two long draws before he decided to say anything. "I gotta be honest with ya, Mick. I don't know if we'll be by for dinner t'morrow. Don't feel much like Thanksgiving right now."

Watching Cry disappear down the dock, Mickey thought about the significant amount of hours they'd spent together over the years. Through high seasons and low seasons, hauling trotlines in a full gale or baitin' and flippin' five hundred pots in a day sometimes, Mickey couldn't imagine a Thanksgiving without Cry Baby.

T-Bone snapped Mickey back to the present. "Alright, thru-hulls are shut – I'm headin' to Grifters." From the dock, he turned back and said, "Yo, Mick – I'm with you on running the string off Bloodsworth. We run to Hooper's Island, we waste half the morning and a ton'a fuel. It was a good bet – ain't yer fault."

***

Letting the truck idle in the gravel lot across from Grifters, Mickey noticed how different the town looked in that particular high-grade autumnal sunshine. Rooflines appeared less crooked, storefronts less vacant, and the streets (although empty) were wide, well-lit, and full of potential. Mickey's waterman town was a brunette of many years suddenly going blonde. It changed her entire face – sadly, it didn't make her any less heavy.

Inside, T-Bone waved a hand and shot a quick whistle. Mickey joined him at the curve of the bar rail and waved a finger to Jo-Jo. All the regulars were in session. An arcane truth bled through the room as each man processed the realities of the past season and postulated on what looked to be an uncertain future.

Across the bar, Grimey George and Payday glossed over as Mayor Pete went on and on with his hopeful delusions about the agricultural port project that the city was trying hard to land. The mayor saw the eighty-acre development as an eagle feather in an otherwise unremarkable cap. Mickey, along with everybody else, caught the tail end of the conversation when the mayor purposely elevated his voice, announcing, "The mission is to lobby those fellas in Washington and Annapolis for the funds. We get a new thirty-foot channel out to deep water and we could handle a million tons of feed grain, vegetables, what-have-you. I'm 'onna tell ya, it's right around the corner – and when it comes, it'll be bigger than the railroad!"

T-Bone leaned in close to Mickey, "You'd think the mayor'd know 'bout the Maryland Wetland Law, right? Ain't no channel bein' dug. 'Sides, they got Baltimore and Norfolk – they don't need us. It's all just a bunch of blowin' smoke and gettin' folks riled up."

"It's quiet here," answered Mickey. "That's why we live here. We don't need a port. We need the Omega plant shut down and cleaner water. We need cold

Novembers for Christ's sake."

"Yessir – and we don't need any more color in this fuckin' town. Things are fine the way they are. We stay outta their way... they stay outta ours. Separate but equal – equally poor." T-Bone laughed and elbowed Mickey, then spun on his stool and marched off to piss. Mickey liked T-Bone well enough but often wondered, sometimes out loud, how anyone in the age of information got anything accomplished, maintaining such a profound and undiluted ignorance.

A firm hand landed on Mickey's back. Tooga sat in T-Bone's place. "Hey, Mick – How'd you do?"

"Great, Toog – had a great season. How's things for you?"

"Aw man, you know. There ain't no shortage of people blowin' up their outboard motors. Got a lotta work. Nobody pay'n me for it, but a lotta work."

Mickey spoke low into the pit of his shoulder, "Lemme ask you something, you still interested in that old Evinrude I got?"

"Your dad's old motor? Shit yeah, but I thought you wadn't ever gonna sell it?"

"Things change, brother. Sometimes the shit's unavoidable." Mickey drained the last of his pint and swirled his empty glass to alert Jo-Jo. "Kaylee needs her inhalers and a dress for the Crab Derby. She's gonna be in the Miss Crustacean Pageant." A smile drew across Mickey's face, then disappeared. "Kim's been workin' her ass off, seven days a week at the salon. I'm sittin' on a World War 2 motor worth three grand. That ain't a sound financial decision."

"Shit, Mickey – I can't pay you what it's worth. I ain't got three grand. He bought that damn thing new in what, like – forty-five?"

"Forty-three," said Mickey, "down at Sterling's Pontiac."

"Goddamn – you know they still have a banner hangin' in the shop advertising the Strato-Streak V-8? That fuckin' motor ain't been made since nineteen-fitty-six."

"Listen, I'll take fifteen for it. Don't say nothin," Mickey paused. "I'd appreciate it – if you kept it 'tween us."

"That ain't no problem. Give my love to Kim and that beautiful little girl a yours." Tooga patted Mickey on the back again before giving T-Bone his stool.

"What ain't no problem?" asked T-Bone. Mickey didn't answer. Jo-Jo placed a full beer down on a fresh coaster in front of Mickey. T-Bone began talking, unconcerned whether there was an audience, spouting off about a desire to exercise his wares on the waitress named Evelyn, completely oblivious to the fact that no woman with a modicum of self-worth would lubricate for a man who announced his presence through a boggy musk of diesel fuel and shellfish and went by the name T-Bone.

Both the sound of T-bone's voice and the noise of the bar began to fade in Mickey's ears. He thought about smoking a cigarette, something he hadn't done since Kaylee was born. He envisioned a night with his family, Kaylee wrestling a pink and green-swirled bowling ball – or the warmth of his wife's hand in a dark theater. Mickey quickly realized that neither of those visions would materialize, as the bowling alley shut down in nineteen-eighty, the movie house was bulldozed in eighty-one to make way for another house of God. Mickey ruminated himself into unswept corners and crevices, shining light into places that had no use for it. He wondered if he'd see Cry Baby for another season, then quickly pivoted to a search for answers as to why Sterling's Pontiac ever felt the need to change; how they used to be all the town needed, one location for boats, farm equipment, and vehicles – before everybody got so specialized – and that maybe he'd a been better at selling cars.

In Mickey's waterman town, the flat economy hung like heavy fog over an exhausted bay, and he knew once the November sunshine was gone and the Thanksgiving atmosphere faded, there'd still be a whole lot of people watching TV in bars at two in the afternoon.

Mickey raced through his beer and piped up to get Jo-Jo's attention. "What do I owe ya?" He threw some dollars on the bar, shook a few hands, and spoke nice words as he made way through a room of liquored-up citizens. A few paces shy of the door, an inebriated T-Bone intercepted him.

"Mick – you leavin'?" T-Bone spoke through a mouthful of taffy.

"Yeah, I gotta get goin' – got people comin' t'morrow. Kim's been on her own all day."

"Aw... you got people. You're a rich man, Mickey Collins!" T-Bone swayed with a rhythm of the reed grass.

"Bones – you ain't driving." Mickey pointed over to Jo-Jo. "Don't you let him –"

"I ain't gonna drive." T-Bone attempted to lift himself on tiptoe, closer to Mickey's face for the conveyance of what he believed to be highly classified information. "Mick, I heard this sayin' one time." T-Bone's combustible words caused Mickey to hold his breath. "Sometimes you're a fox and sometimes – you're the fuckin' chicken. Sump'n like that. You understand what I'm sayin', don't cha?"

"I do bud, thank you. You are a true gentleman and a scholar."

"A what? I'm drunk, I know – but I'm just sayin, Mick – things gonna be alright. We're fuckin' watermen."

"We are watermen, Bones. And with some luck and the right weather, we get to try again next year."

An Interview

Please, come in.
May I take your coat?
Coffee?

I must admit, I was a bit shocked when you said you wrote for a newspaper. There aren't many of you left. Forgive me, the name again?

Mm, the Democrat-Gazette – Little Rock?

You don't say. Amazing to think there's a Democrat anywhere near Arkansas these days. Before we start, I should warn you, I've been having a great debate with myself since we last spoke. This story's been buried for a long time. People have moved on, started over. And while the utopian in me wants to believe in the benefits of tearing open such wounds, the utilitarian knows better and strongly suggests we let sleeping dogs lie. Should a look of sudden perplexity become apparent in my expression during our conversation, I assure you it's not a coronary episode. I'm merely chastising myself for letting you in.

Please, have a seat.

You look very young to me. Then again, everyone looks young to me these days. I'm sure you're not too young to be unfamiliar with Hippocrates, at least in name alone?

Good. I'll go on then – of course, with the knowledge that it's never a good strategy to begin with Hippocrates. But, as it pertains to the forthcoming discussion, I feel it's important to note that he had a theory. Hippocrates believed the condition was caused by an imbalance in the child's makeup; too much fire and not enough water. By today's parameters, it's absurd in its medicine, but significant for one reason: that in the age of Hippocrates, such a condition existed at all. What's also significant – to me – is that nothing further was written about it until 1943, when Kanner published his landmark paper on Affective Contact. Sadly, he provided us all with an equally absurd description, calling the condition an anxiously-obsessive desire for the maintenance of sameness. With explanations such as these, it's no wonder we meandered for so long with our heads up our asses. All of this to say, it took until the late 1980s before the mental health community finally revised and simplified the diagnosis into something people could grasp. Before that, kids like Nicholas simply fell through the cracks.

I should admit, as a young pediatrician fresh out of residency at the time, a portion of the blame for the boy's misconduct, misdiagnosis, and misfortune might land squarely on my shoulders. Back then, I marched with heavy steps through the quicksand of absolute certainty. In case you don't know, there's no shortage of ego in young doctors. Now, I'm not quite so pigheaded, but I'll let you be the judge of that. If you'll allow me to consult my notes as we move along, I'll apologize in advance. I haven't spoken about this in decades, and I want to get the story straight – for Nicholas.

More coffee?

Okay then – How would you like me to begin?

Okay.

Anthony Bevilaqua and I met at the Folcroft Swim Club, summer of '76. I was Chairman of the Board, Anthony became my co-chair. Community pools had yet to fall out of fashion. The AIDS epidemic was still a few years off – child abductions and school shootings were Orwellian concoctions. They didn't happen in Overbrook Park. Like most of America, we were dealing with the fallout, trying to figure out the best way to reintegrate damaged young men returning from Vietnam. They were difficult days. Nixon was gone, but so were the Beatles.

Anthony and his wife were very active at the club. Whenever help was needed, Anthony, Joan, and the three kids were there. Young Nicholas was always a handful, behaving like a ten-year-old boy – or worse. Cathy and Paul were, by all outward appearances, much calmer. In their mid-teens, they were entering an entirely new stage of mischief, one that could do real harm. They required all available resources. You can understand where that left Nicholas.

I'm sorry – I don't mean to laugh. You asked about the first time I met Nicholas, and I was struck remembering. His father and I had just won a year-long battle with the board, getting them to release the funds needed to replace our chalky, aluminum diving boards with modern fiberglass. Some of the members suggested doing away with them altogether. They were well ahead of Anthony and me in their fears of an increasingly litigious society. But, Anthony and I flexed our muscles and... I'm sorry, I'm rambling – do you have enough tape on that thing?

Digital – of course. Where was I?

Diving boards – thank you.

The boy couldn't have been more than ten years old up there, hands clasped at his chin, purple lips quivering, knock-kneed and pigeon-toed. The poor kid was terrified. The other children had already retreated to the cafeteria and were well into eating the place through from sole plate to shingle, watching Nicholas' misfortune unfold a hundred feet away.

He was a cerebral kid, Nicholas – not the athlete that Paul was. He kept to himself. I think Anthony had a great deal of trouble relating to the boy. I remember him yelling, "Goddammit Nicholas – it's ten feet for Christ's sake!" It was perfectly clear, the only way Nicholas would be dismissed – allowed to join the other kids – would be if he jumped. The sooner he got the nonsense over with, the sooner he'd eat.

I will tell you – Nicholas wasn't afraid of his father's Parris Island bluster. The boy stood on that board for the better part of an hour. When Anthony finally relented and agreed to let Nicholas back down the ladder, he jumped! Not only that, by the time the bubbles cleared, the kid was mid-way down the pool, underwater on a single breath. He finally surfaced – shot out like a rainbow trout – didn't say a word. He just took off, ran all the way home – three miles, barefoot.

The change?

I noticed a change the summer he turned twelve. Anthony mentioned some difficulty at school but promptly dismissed it as little more than the normal growing pains of a twelve-year-old vying for position in the middle-school pecking order. I suspected something different, but it wasn't my place. Back then, we were less inclined to stick our nose in places than people are today. Things deteriorated quickly. At least once a week, there was a fight on the playground. Nicholas bore the brunt of it. "Nicholas," they'd say, "You have to stop being so weird." Kids can be so cruel. Adults can be worse.

By the time he entered the eighth grade, Nicholas rarely spoke. Oftentimes only to me and mostly to the subject of wormholes, time machines, and, as he put it, the indisputable fourth dimension. I simply tried my best to keep up, nodding my head and uttering things like, "That's incredible, Nicholas," and, "You don't say."

Because he refused to speak, his grades suffered. He was continuously reprimanded and endlessly bullied. When he did speak, he was punished. When he refused to speak because he feared being punished, he was punished. You see? The irony, the cruelty... Mm.

At home, it was the quintessential decline. Anthony became a first-rate drunk. Joan, weary of explaining the black eyes, disappeared for days on end. Quietly, over the issue of Nicholas, our little community separated like oil from water.

Spring of '78 – I decided to intervene and had a brief amount of luck on a day when Anthony was generously guilt-ridden. He agreed to let a specialist examine Nicholas. And, as suspected, he went well beyond the testing ceilings of other twelve-year-olds, so much so that the Yale School of Medicine offered to pay for Nicholas' expenses if Anthony would agree to let him visit and test in their program. My interference caused a great confrontation and ultimately ended any remaining friendship I had with Anthony. He prevented me from ever seeing Nicholas again. He prevented anyone from seeing Nicholas. What other outcome could we have expected?

I'm sorry, that was inappropriate.

I believe we've reached the point – where I regret agreeing to this.

Let's cut to the quick, shall we? You've listened, patiently, as I've gone on about my relationship with Nicholas, sat quietly while I questioned my handling of the matter for the thousandth time. You've twisted the cap of that pen for nearly twenty minutes. I may be old – however, I am keenly aware that you haven't come all this way for a dissertation on behavioral psychology or my thoughts on autism.

So – in the interest of time, why don't you just ask me – if I think Nicholas killed those boys. I'll wait.

Turn that off.

Well, if you want me to answer your question... turn it off.

Those boys terrorized Nicholas his entire seventh and eighth-grade years. I had to set his arm – twice. They kicked him so hard on one occasion... are you aware of the trauma that needs to occur to cause brain swelling?

As I feared, this has taken me down a path I had no desire to walk again. I would like it to stop.

Young man, I've devoted my entire life to the betterment of others, and I'm proud of that. But it's come at a price. You see, sometimes knowing things is bittersweet. At first, the successful diagnosis comes as a relief. You've figured it out, solved the problem. Good show, my boy! Here's your medal. Then comes the recognition of missed opportunities; how much damage would have been prevented if our social conscience made allowances for those with misdiagnosed mental illnesses. We've lost an entire generation of souls – through the cracks – and I've been trying to live with that.

I'm sorry I've wasted your time. I'll get your coat.

Missed Opportunities

The Lake Maggiore neighborhood on St. Petersburg's south end was seeing something of a resurgence. Expanding along with its gator population was Lake Maggiore's favorability among young families looking to enjoy all that the city had to offer, but fell a few chai lattes shy of the median income requirements of Old Northeast.

Not too long ago, before Ronald Reagan, the old-growth neighborhood would have been considered walkable from the downtown waterfront district. Today, those afflicted with the disease of modern convenience might wholeheartedly disagree. The lake itself was a geometric conundrum. To someone unfamiliar with it, a close approximation might be had by describing a Dorito after a considerable amount of time floating in a swimming pool.

The heavily decomposed body was discovered at its northeastern point, where Salt Creek enters from Tampa Bay. Local police arrived after a caller reported an alligator dragging what appeared to be a body through the mangroves. Crouching police officers wrestled and duck-crawled their way through dense vegetation with a hand cupped over their nose and mouth and a twitching eye out for the gators that submerged upon arrival of the fire rescue boats. A hundred yards away, the county sheriff, along with additional uniformed officials from Florida Fish and Wildlife, stood guard over a mound of covered remains.

Outside a perimeter cordoned off with fluorescent tape, an Action News reporter held a recording device to the chin of a sixty-three-year-old local man.

"I seen a gator chomping it. My wife Emma and I eat breakfast here every morning. We was eatin' crackers and bologna – I saw it in the mangroves. That damn thing took a bite, threw it in the air and caught it in its mouth! I videoed it – den I called the police." The young reporter went pale watching the video and choked down bile in her throat.

Nearby, an officer waved the camo-painted F-350 of Mike and Sissy Clayton through the barricade. As the only husband-and-wife team of gator wranglers in Pinellas County, or any Florida county for that matter, Mike and Sissy were the first call when nuisance gators wandered into backyards, swimming pools, or onto country club golf courses. Additionally, when partially-devoured bodies were spotted floating in Lake Maggiore.

Mike Clayton was a hulk of a man with a physique optimized for two specific purposes: special operations and gator wrangling. Sissy was his exact and comical opposite, barely taller than the behemoth Ford's tailgate in its fully reclined position. Outside the truck, Mike holstered his Hellcat 9mm and snatched a backpack from the cab. Sissy met him at the driver's side, carrying a small duffle. The muscular duo crossed the embankment dressed in khaki tactical pants and black polos embossed with *Total Control's* logo.

Mike gestured to Sheriff Frank Wilkes, who was standing by the remains talking into a phone. He squatted and raised the plastic tarp high enough to examine the damage; the humid stench wrecked his face. Sissy rested a palm on each shoulder and gazed over Mike's broad back.

"Jesus Christ – that's been out here a while," she said.

"Looky-there, a Hollywood sock. That's sump'n we don't see every day."

Sheriff Wilkes ended his call, squatted next to Mike and Sissy, and said, "Another day or so, wouldn't be nothing left to find."

"Why isn't Harvey here?" asked Mike.

"He's on his way. I'm sure he'll run a tox screen, but – no tellin' what he'll find with the body in this condition."

"That arrest bracelet should tell him the identity. Then you just gotta figure out if it's foul play."

"The mayor is losing his shit over this. It's the third gator attack in the last month."

"Woah, Frank – you don't know this was a gator attack. All you've got is part of a body. A body we can't even identify as male or female. There's nothing indicating this was an attack – it could've been dumped here. A gator's a gator. It's gonna eat, and it don't give a damn what it eats or how it got there." Mike ran a hand down the length of his sandy beard. "I'd hold off callin' this a gator incident until you find out more 'bout that bracelet."

"Well if I were you, Mike, I'd kill something – quick. String it up, take a picture. Make

the mayor happy. The Pride Parade's in two weeks."

"Frank, I'm gonna tell you something, and you aren't gonna be happy 'bout it." Mike

paused, rethinking his decision to disclose what he was thinking. "The gator that made the marks on that body ain't in this lake."

Sheriff Frank stood up and spat. "What are you saying?"

"I'm saying – that the gators here in Maggiore run about seven, eight foot. They ain't gonna mess with a full-sized person. Look at the bite radius on that body – it's a twelve-footer, and that ain't no shit."

Whenever Mike or Sissy was asked to discuss the upticks in gator interactions with people and pets, their answers usually resulted in hurt feelings. Mike took great pride in eviscerating the facades of local government officials dispensing 'thoughts and prayers' in front of news cameras. And those people rarely enjoyed when Mike used identifying prefixes such as negligent, irresponsible, feckless, and greedy. The blame, Mike Clayton believed, could be placed at the feet of interlopers such as city commissioners turned politicians or politicians turned developers. Either way, Mike's position on the matter was crystal clear: human encroachment into wildlife habitats almost always resulted in things dying.

Sissy's phone rang. She listened for a few seconds then said, "Okay, darlin'. We'll be right there."

Harbortown Marina was approximately two miles from Maggiore by F-350. It was less than a mile by Salt Creek, but the cut-through between the two was nearly impassable for anything larger than a kayak, overgrown with a tangled mess of mangroves, scrub oak, and cabbage palms. In the early 1930s, the city had a master plan to connect Tampa Bay with Boca Ciega via Salt Creek and Lake Maggiore. That plan ended shortly after the initial phase of construction flooded the lake with saltwater, killing everything in it. For decades since, anglers have been bellyaching about the inconveniences they've had to endure in their pursuit of abusing creatures of nature and authorized beer sluggery. Disallowing the cutting of mangroves in the Salt Creek passthrough was just another attempt at keeping the man down.

As Harbortown's dockmaster for the better part of two decades, Brad Taylor was a native Floridian who managed to keep his position even after hurricane Andrew, two economic collapses, and three management changes. At the present moment, he was pulling out what little hair remained on his square head as the marina was at the tail end of a twenty-million-dollar rehab. One that saw an expansion into the north harbor and the construction of floating concrete docks with the ability to accommodate vessels big enough to be owned by sheiks and various Fortune 500 philanderers.

Brad peered down at Mike and Sissy from the mezzanine and waved a hand for them to come on up. "Thanks for coming," he said, hugging Sissy, shaking Mike's gigantic hand. "How's it going over there – any news?"

"The body's still layin' in the grass," Sissy said. "Everybody wants to call it an attack, but we don't think it was gator related." She motioned for Mike to continue and put her hands on her hips.

"What you need to know right now is – there's a big gator 'round here, man. I'm talking twelve foot. This area ain't seen anything that big in twenty years. You might wanna caution your divers."

Brad closed the office door. "It's here, in the marina." He sat behind his desk with a heavy sense of dread.

"Where?" asked Mike.

"J-dock – in the mud, just below the drainpipe at the generator station." Brad propped his elbows on the desk, interlocked his fingers under his chin, and said, "I got the owner of the New York Knicks on A-dock. Bill Edward's boat is across from him, and the Sternbergs are coming tomorrow. I can't have this shit right now."

"Well Brad, I don't know who any of those people are, but I'm assuming they're important." Mike added a smile in an attempt to inject a note of levity into the moment.

"Important... rich and powerful. If one of their Shih

Tzus gets snatched off the dock, this marina will go away." Brad stood up. "Can you handle this without making a mess?"

Sissy said, "We've been doing this a long time. We'll run a bait trail to draw this old boy back to Maggiore. You won't see anything, but you might smell the bait if the wind shifts."

"When?"

"Tonight."

***

The plan was to launch the skiff and enter the marina shortly after dark on a rising tide. With the near-silent electric motor, Mike and Sissy could travel the four-foot deep drainage channel virtually undetected by marina guests. The run between J-dock and the dense embankment was, by Mike's guess, two-hundred yards to the connection with Salt Creek, and then another half-mile to the passthrough at the lake entrance. While they much preferred daylight for this exercise, Mike and Sissy kept the task simple: set bait poles and get out.

Mike carried the Hellcat on his hip and shouldered a Sig .45. Sissy wore her 9mm in a holster at the small of her back. Bang sticks, harpoons, bait wire, and half-a-dozen bamboo poles were loaded into the twelve-foot boat. Mike stepped aboard, carrying a thirty-gallon Rubbermaid tote holding clear bait bags containing his usual preparation of pig lungs and beef hearts that had been left to rot for a few days in the blazing Florida sun.

Bloated from the noxious gasses, Mike and Sissy handled the bags as if they were nitroglycerin balloons.

The moon hung like a Chinese lantern over the Coast Guard station. They made good time to the marina; the skiff helped along by the gentle flooding tide they were looking to ride. Drifting past the drainpipe where Brad last spotted the gator, Sissy's stomach began to turn. She lost her focus, something that was becoming a semi-regular occurrence. Sissy's woolgathering often coincided with highly stressful moments, and usually landed her in similar moments from her past; say, for instance, the car accident that left her with a broken back, which resulted in the loss of her athletic scholarship. When she'd arrive back from her momentary departures, there was a great deal of confusion regarding the amount of time she'd been absent. There were instances when Sissy'd drive from one place to the next without remembering a single minute of the trip. She refrained from mentioning any of this to Mike – especially now – considering where they were and what they were about to undertake.

"Sissy!" Mike snapped in a low voice. "What the hell, baby? I've asked you three times to hand me that pole."

"I'm sorry. I was thinking 'bout something... here."

Where the drainage channel merged with Salt Creek, Mike sank the first eight-foot pole into the mud. He cut a bag open and gagged at the putrid liquid spilling into the creek. Sissy spat over the side.

"Goddamn," Mike said. "That old boy's gonna pick this scent up real quick."

This first pole would only contain a bloody beef heart, no hooks. A teaser, easy prey to lure a beast upriver and away from the marina. The second pole was rigged the same way – just a bit further along. For the third set, Sissy piloted the skiff into the overhanging brush east of the passthrough. Mike wanted to hang the last rig in the camouflage of the scrub oak at the entrance of the lake. It was a hard place to see from the road or the marina. If there was a ruckus, it could be contained.

Attached to a length of braided stainless steel wire was a swivel with fifty feet of heavy cord, and a weighted treble hook the size of Sissy's hand. Mike sunk the hooks deep into the set of oozing pig lungs and positioned the spinning mess to dangle two feet above the surface of the water. Once underneath, the gator'd raise himself out of the water and hit hard, swallowing the contraption deep into its gut.

The trip back to the launch ramp was all but silent. Inside the truck, illuminated by the dome light, Mike addressed Sissy's fade-away. "You alright?"

"Yeah, baby. I'm sorry. I just drifted off. It won't happen again."

"I'm worried 'bout you. Why don't you take tomorrow – do something fun. I'll ask Chaz to help me wrap this up. Hell, he might not hit that hook tonight – could be a day or two."

"Baby, I'm fine. He's gonna hit it. This'll be over tomorrow – then maybe you and me both can go down to Pine Island or Lorelei's for the weekend." Sissy leaned across the console, plucked scrub oak debris from his beard, then kissed his mouth.

***

Mike and Sissy were back at the boat ramp early enough to make long, bending shadows in the rise of an apricot sun. For this mission, Mike towed the better-equipped eighteen-foot jon boat. Standing on the bow, he took inventory – .45 bang stick, snag hooks, harpoons, extra line, and the 12 gauge.

Sissy drove the boat through a weightless morning breeze, the smell of creosote and roasted coffee fluttering over the skiff. They talked about what they'd always talked about before a big hunt – the details. If the hooked bait was gone, the gator was more than likely on the bottom, dying slowly from a bleeding gut. Mike would slowly haul in the line. Sissy would stand by with the loaded bang stick. If Mike was successful at reeling the gator close to the boat, the chances of a riot breaking out were high. The hope was the old boy'd be close to dead and down on his strength. Mike never counted on hope.

If he could keep a hold throughout the gator's ragging spins, Sissy could get a bang stick into the kill zone on the back of his head, just behind the eyes. Done correctly, one shot would do it. A thick skull usually kept the shot from blowing out the throat and ruining what stood to be a very valuable hide. They'd done it a hundred times, but Sissy liked to talk through it as if it were the first.

Rounding the corner into the drainage channel, the sun climbed above the mangroves. Sissy felt its warmth on her back. Passing the drainpipe, the first pole came into view. Only the top six inches were visible above the water at a low angle. Mike held a palm up to Sissy and she slowed the motor. In a wide stance, Mike gently snatched it using a fiberglass pole with a blunt hook at its end. The bait wire was clean. Sissy broke a small smile and held up her index finger.

They found the same at the second pole. The gator had taken the bait. The next turn would reveal if the hooked bait had been swallowed as well. Sissy killed the engine. The boat's momentum carried it around the bend. The bait was gone. The line was taut.

Mike donned a pair of sweat-stained leather gloves. "There ain't much room in here. We don't want this ol' boy dragging us into the passthrough. That happens, I'll pay out the line, you back us out – set a stern anchor. Then we'll pull him to us."

Sissy nodded in agreement, loaded a single .45 caliber shell into the bang stick, and laid it at her feet. She broke open the shotgun across her knee and thumbed one shell up top and one in the second barrel; clipped it shut. She chambered a round in her Hellcat and holstered it.

"Ready, baby?"

"I'm ready," Sissy replied.

Mike began to reel in on the line, careful not to let it coil around his feet. He felt an immense mass on the third pull, like a waterlogged oak stump skidding through the mud. Sissy's jaw clenched, she stood like an ancient Greek figure with the five-foot-long bang stick at the ready. They exchanged glances, but nothing was said. Mike kept steady pressure. The water was less than six feet. *Where are you*, he thought. Seconds later, the massive head broke the water's surface, the pungent smell of rotting meat and cat piss caused him to hold his breath.

"Shit! He's facing the wrong way."

The massive gator thrashed, nearly jerking Mike off the bow. The hook was deep. The line exited the corner of his mouth. Mike had to be careful not to pull his guts out as the gator spun and crashed his thick skull into the aluminum boat.

"I can't get around you. I got no shot!" Sissy shouted. "Hand me the line – take the stick."

"No... he'll pull you in."

Mike strained to keep the gator's head up. The jaws opened wide and snapped shut with a mechanical energy. He pulled hard against the line and dove under, dragging the boat towards the mangroves, just as Mike feared.

"Toss the hook!"

Sissy heaved the anchor over the stern and cleated the bitter end. Mike fended off scrub oak branches and prickly palm fronds, keeping tension on the line. Sissy had clear air space at the back of the boat.

"Can you pull us back?" asked Mike with heavy breaths.

Sissy hauled in on the anchor line. The boat drifted back. Mike suggested switching places and directed Sissy to take the bow. He stepped lightly over the benches and took a wider stance, low in the center of the boat.

"Okay, Sis... we're gonna try this again. When he

comes up, hit that head."

Mike pulled in the line. The gator's head broke the surface again. This time, Sissy had the angle. She plunged the bang stick. There was a dull crack and a puff of light blue smoke. The gator recoiled, thrust himself upward into the hull, knocking Sissy backward. She needed two hands to keep from going in. Sissy watched the silver pole sink. Mike fell hard into the outboard with a loud gasp. Bands of sunlight dappled the water, illuminating a brick red discharge from the gator's mouth.

"His eyes are still open – he ain't dead. Hit 'em again!"

"I lost the stick. It went over when I fell."

"Don't use your sidearm. I don't want you reaching over the boat. Get the shotgun."

Sissy lunged for the gun; the gator's snout was just above the gunwale of the boat. On her knees at the bow once again, Sissy clicked off the safety and pressed the barrel into the kill spot.

"Go!" Mike shouted.

The moment Mike shouted, the gator spun his enormous bulk, thrusting the barrel skyward. Sissy fired. The kick of the shotgun knocked her backward. Mike went airborne over the rail. Sissy scampered to the back of the boat, screaming Mike's name. Her hoarse shrieks reached a panic pitch when she saw the damage to his cranium and the amount of blood pouring out of her husband.

Sissy gasped, her brain grappling for good decisions. She did what they'd always talked about never doing – she panicked. Sissy jumped, swam to Mike's body, and pulled him by the pant cuff to the boat. Hysterical, trying to heave his massive, lifeless body into the boat, she went under again and again. Crying and struggling to breathe, her chin just above the surface, Sissy felt the heavy impact in her midsection. She heard a dull crunch and felt the vertebrae in her spine compress. The air left her chest in a long exhale as she was pulled under. Peering up through the magenta water, she watched a trio of small bubbles drift to the surface and release the last of her breath into the glowing light of a glorious summer morning; something Sissy realized she'd never see again.

Hooligan

Have you ever burned down a bank? I suppose, neither have I. Sure, I reeked of smoke when I finally arrived home that afternoon, but it was more than likely from the Marlboro reds I stole from the Wawa on Burmont Road. That's what I've been telling myself, anyway – for decades. It was the cigarettes.

And that was pretty much the extent of it, my hooligan expertise – petty theft. Stealing cigarettes, chucking snowballs at cars from the roof of the Exxon station, and laying batteries on the trolley tracks. Amateur mischief, not the professional sort of shit that leads to mug-shots and neck tattoos.

For most of the day – before the bank burned down – Billy and I were nowhere near the place. It was one of those white-elephant days in Philly when the

Delaware County School Board was satisfied that a sufficient amount of snow had fallen to justify giving the little fuckers off. Billy and I double-bagged our feet, courtesy of Wonder Bread, and headed for the epic sledding hill behind the Drexelbrook Apartments. A hill that would, if you missed the turn at the telephone pole, shoot you airborne into midday traffic or the side of a Septa bus waiting to swallow bundled-up Catholic women on their way to mass.

Yes, we were sledding on lunch trays stolen from our school cafeteria, but we'd made off with those long before. It no longer counted toward our delinquency credits. Only an hour or so passed before the winter day soaked through our acid-washed Levis and chilled us to the point our lips quivered without permission. We decided to call it a day, but not before stopping for a brief respite in the abandoned bank.

We didn't even have to kick in the louvered door, as an earlier group of underachievers beat us to it. Its insides looked the way an abandoned building is supposed to look. The ransacked space appeared apocalyptic with its overturned desks and file cabinets strewn about. Wires dangled from the drop ceiling. The peeling linoleum was hidden under a damp carpet, ankle-deep in ledgers, blank envelopes, and the sorted paperwork appropriate to banks. All of its orphaned dankness aggravated by the cold of the day. Despite what you may be thinking, there was indeed a modicum of sensible brain activity occurring between us. There had to be, or we never would have started the fire.

Billy said, "What's better, a king or a duke?"

"A king – dipshit."

"I heard Ozzy bit the head off a bat – ain't that fucked up?"

"Well, Jamie told me Kelly Whitmore gave Tommy a hand-job in study-hall."

We laughed and laughed, smoked the last of the Marlboros, and coaxed new life into our frozen hands over a modest flame. We paid little attention to the flecks of feather-like ash as they cooled from glowing orange to slate gray and floated into frostbitten rafters. Untold sagacious thinkers have spent countless hours pontificating around bonfires from Darkan to Detroit, yet no one can competently explain the elation that males, be they fifteen or fifty, feel when extinguishing a fire with a piss stream.

Feeling the day's mischief was championship quality, I burst through the door to apartment 3A to find my mother standing in front of the TV, drying her hands on a plaid dishtowel. I peeled off the layers and dropped them where I stood.

"You're late. Where ya been?" she asked on her way by.

"Sledding, with Billy."

She handed me a plate. The aromas of sweet garlic and oregano wafted from a mound of angel-hair smothering two meatballs and a toasted kaiser roll saturated with melted garlic butter; all of it drenched in my mother's translucent marinara. My mom sat across from me with a plate half the size.

"Did'juh have fun?"

I nodded and mumbled through a mouthful.

"It's so sad," she added, twisting pasta around a fork, shaking her head.

"What?" I said, not looking up.

"That old bank, the one over by Billy's house, it's on fire. Garrett Road's shut down... three alarms." Then, she popped a perfect blob of pasta into her mouth.

I tried to control my reaction, but I was woefully unsuccessful. I coughed so violently I upset the entire table. In my defense, it wasn't a particularly sturdy table, mind you. Rather a lightly-built thing with folding legs and a faux leather surface. You know, to add a bit of opulence to the Monday night bridge game. Nonetheless, I knocked over my milk and her stemmed glass of Paul Masson, of course, ruining the entire meal.

"Oh – Charlie," she said, calmer than she should have been.

"Shit!"

"Charlie! Goddamn it. What did I say about cursing?"

Without ever connecting the dots that almost anyone but my mother would have connected, she cleared plates and began mopping up the crime scene, concealing her exasperation. "Go get cleaned up," she said. "You smell like smoke."

I felt the blood tingle in my feet. I couldn't tell if it was from the frostbite subsiding or pure fear, and I made the grave mistake of making eye contact when my mother glared at me.

"Charlie," she said, ceasing all activity – doing that

mom thing – standing with a fist on each hip. I swear it was Clint Eastwood's voice I heard when she said, "Is there something you wanna tell me (punk)?"

Suddenly, I was watching a movie, outside my body. I could see it playing out from afar, from a position in the kitchen hovering just above the stove, and I wanted to shout to myself, "Charlie – close your fuckin mouth!" But, I didn't. I stood there with my mouth open, just wide enough for a ping pong ball. In answer to her question, I said no. But I wasn't convincing. I whispered. It sounded like a question.

"Don't lie to me," said Clint. "Were you smoking?"

I might have peed a little when I gasped. "Yeah – yes, I did... was... I smoked." And then, as most guilty men do, I began talking too much and too fast, offering up unsolicited information – mercy-of-the-court type shit. "Billy bought 'em. I only had one... I hated it... it made me choke. I'm sorry, mom. I'm sorry."

And just like that, she pulled me into her bosom, her chin pressed into the crown of my head. While I could hardly breathe, I didn't dare pull away, risk further eye contact, and an almost certain connecting of the dots.

Quarantine

East to west was probably the best vantage point if you wanted to see that afternoon sky over the city. Various shades of pink and orange not visible on any color wheel hovered over apocalyptic empty streets. No taxis, no trash, no wind. Not a single person. The cacophonous heartbeat that once ripped through the city like a flatbed jazz band was gone. Sole proof of life – a pigeon, battering its wings against the sky, sounding an alarm to no one. April 1 and months of business – the entire spring and summer seasons – vanished in seven simple days. It was no joke.

Danny leaned with two hands on an empty bar. Over his shoulder, a muted broadcast displayed a news lady miming the latest updates. A man entered through the front door that Danny forgot to lock.

"Hey, Gar... we're closed man. They catch me serving anyone, I'll get fined."

"Seriously – just one? I only got six bucks." Gary paused, holding the door open, half inside and half out. "I just got laid off. Vicki threw me out."

Danny usually met discomfort shortly following the moments in which he led with his heart. He'd given up any hope of becoming the kind of callused, self-preserved bastard that seemed to flourish in downturns.

"Fuck it. C'mon... and lock that door, will ya? This quarantine shit's gonna shut me down anyway. What's the difference." Danny wiped his mouth with the back of his hand. "What're ya having?"

"What'll six bucks buy me?"

"Tonight? You're in luck, my friend," said Danny, killing the TV's signal with the remote. "Two for one – just started."

"Jameson?"

"Yessir."

Danny set a double pour on a napkin for Gary and poured one for himself. The two men tapped glasses and drank.

Danny said, "You wanna talk about it?" Gary shook his head. "That's what I figured."

"She won't quit spending money. She's got a credit card for Victoria's Secret. I dunno who's benefitin' from that shit, but sure as *hell* ain't me – goddamn it." Gary interrupted himself, swallowed his full pour.

"I thought you didn't want to talk about it."

"I don't," said Gary tersely, changing the subject. "You really gonna have to shut down?"

"I'm on the knife's edge here, man. I can't afford to go dark for a month." Danny refilled their glasses. "I ain't caught up from 2008. Everybody said I needed to add food. I added food. You know what happens when you add food? You add a cook. Then, you gotta add a fuckin' dishwasher. It's just me and Kelly tending the bar, and I sent her home in tears. Who's gonna pay her rent?" Danny emptied his glass. "This ain't Wall Street down here. Ain't nobody bailin' my ass out. We get sick, we're screwed. Hell, even if we don't get sick – we're screwed."

Gary held his glass with two hands. "Yeah, it's pretty fucked up."

"Listen, I ain't kicking you out, but – I gotta kick you out." Danny poured one more for the both of them and immediately drained his. Gary slapped six tattered dollar bills on the bar and slid them under his palm. Danny waved him off. "It's on the house. Take it while I got one."

"I don't know where I'm supposed to go."

"You're supposed to go home, Gar. Go home. Fix it. Shit's about to get real. You're gonna need Vicki. And, regardless a'what she thinks, she's gonna need you."

"Honestly," said Gary. "I don't know what I'd do without her."

"Well, my friend. I have a feeling we're all about to learn what we can do without."

Endings and Beginnings

The day's sunshine had faded. The sky transitioned from flamingo pink to eggplant. A woman talked into her phone, illuminated by intermittent flashes of amber coming from the Tacoma idling on the Brawley overpass.

"Hey Wayne, it's Linda. Oh, I'm fine, but Joe – he ain't so good. You might wanna send an ambulance over to the house."

She was desert slim with a thicket of shoulder-length strawberry hair that more than adequately covered the swelling in her face and an eye tinged with blood. "I don't *think* he's dead..." she said in a salty voice, "...but I wouldn't bet a kidney or anything on that." She uttered two "uh-huh's," then said, "Sheriff, I'm not coming back, and if you'd relay that message – I'd appreciate it." Satisfied with everything she wanted to say, Linda Blanton leaned her shoulders over the guardrail, extended her arm, and spread her fingers wide apart. Her stylish smartphone plummeted thirty feet, splashed into the New River, and sunk.

Linda checked her mirrors for any approaching cars or trucker rigs, killed the flashers, and accelerated south on Route 111. If a cast iron skillet to the head had resulted in depriving her husband of any more life, she knew someone would be coming for her. While she had fantasized about the bastard's demise once or twice in the past, she enjoyed very much existing on the free side of a prison fence. Being that there was no way to know her husband's current condition, she began to fear the highway and decided to take the Anza turnoff and continue on surface roads.

Too late in the day for a border crossing, she remembered an old motor lodge in Heber. The low-slung motel rated highly among truckers and adulterers for two reasons: homemade buttermilk biscuits and rooms that opened directly into the parking lot, thereby absolving any guilty party by allowing them to circumvent any direct contact with desk clerks and surveillance cameras. For Linda, it would do as an adequate bolthole for the night.

Sheriff Wayne Ramirez responded to the call, as both his deputy and lieutenant were holding a suspicious tractor-trailer that blew a weigh station on 86 just outside Brawley, quite possibly in sight of the overpass. Still chewing the amorphous details of Linda's call, the sheriff radioed Imperial County's paramedic unit to meet him at the Blanton residence.

Sheriff Ramirez turned onto Orban Road from its southern end where it intersected 4th Street. The paramedic unit came from the north, and the two vehicles with competing lights met at the entrance to Joe and Linda's driveway, a place they'd been before. Ramirez flashed his hi-beams for the paramedics to go ahead, figuring Joe's heartbeat could fade at any moment if it hadn't already.

Earlier that morning at the Buckshot Diner, the sheriff detected nothing out of the ordinary when Joe spun from a stool at the counter and pecked Linda on the cheek before heading off to his position of management at Niland's Recycling Renter. After which, Linda slid a warm plate cradling the sheriff's circadian breakfast special across the table with her usual blithe disposition. It's worth noting, the sheriff usually lost the ability to detect anything once the split biscuit covered in hash browns, chorizo patty, and fried egg slathered in white gravy arrived.

Joe Blanton was on all fours in front of the KitchenAide, bleeding profusely from the nose and other areas, a bag of frozen snap beans wrapped in a dish towel to the side of his face. A single burner, cooking nothing but the evening breeze, heated the stove grate to glowing red. From the looks of things, salmon was on the menu. The shrapnel of long-grain rice and caramelized asparagus marked the walls and ceiling. To Linda's good fortune, her husband was alive – at least for the moment.

Paramedics attributed Joe's garbled speech to a combination of things: fractured skull and cheekbone, some busted teeth, and a heavy dose of whatever fermentation was burning their eyes. Joe said some things, but the sheriff – being naturally resistant to the obvious conclusions – was still unclear as to what exactly transpired, as almost all of Joe's words were indecipherable nonsense. Sheriff Ramirez decided it probably wasn't the best time to relay the message about his wife not coming back.

***

Linda overestimated the competence of law enforcement agencies when it came to conveying pertinent information and arrived at the border crossing before daybreak. Consumed with the realization she might be a fugitive kept her awake most of the night. That amount of perceived guilt caused her to tremble and stutter when the Mexican border guard began asking routine questions.

"Buenos Dias. Habla Español?"

"Um, no... not well anyway."

"Where are you going?" asked the uniformed female. Leaning herself closer to the driver's side window, she scanned the truck's interior waiting for Linda to answer.

"Ensenada... for a couple days – vacation – sort of." Linda diverted her eyes, leaned her head at an awkward angle to hide the damaged side of her face, which had begun to show pale yellows and varying degrees of purple.

"Do you need medical attention?"

"Oh... no – this?" Linda leaned out the window to see her reflection in a side mirror. "This happened a couple weeks ago. I fell... fell off my horse. You shoulda seen it then." She added a chuckle.

The agent looked aft and said, "I need to see in the back." Linda walked the soldier and her machine gun to the rear bumper and opened the cab window, revealing an empty truck bed.

"American woman... going on vacation with no luggage?" The guard's eyes locked in on Linda's face.

"I have a backpack up front. I got everything I need." She hadn't intended to slam the glass on the truck cab when she closed it.

"Park over there. Immigration is through those doors. Bienvenidos, welcome to Mexico." The words were unemotional, encased in a patina of pleasantness reserved for weekend migrators.

Back in the driver's seat, Linda's heartbeat quickened as she crept through Mexicali's crowded, narrow streets. At the first opportunity, she turned south on a less traveled road, her tight grip on the wheel eased with the morning sun touching the side of her face. Without any exact knowledge of where she was driving, she steered the Tacoma into the dusty lot of a small tienda, pressed the crown of her head into the headrest, and breathed a heavy sigh. The events of the last twelve hours arrived in her body. In an effort to tamp down the urge to crack open, Linda decided to think about practical things. She scribbled a small list on the back of the immigration regulations. At the top, the first thing – was to find out if she'd killed her husband.

A gimped street dog followed Linda as far as the threshold of the store and stopped. In the back corner, next to a bin of dusty onions and sprouting garlic, she located a coffee pot and poured out its sludged, hours-old brew. She gathered up a three-liter jug of drinking water, two packs of powdered mini-donettes, the English version of Guia Roji's Mexican Road Atlas, and from the woman at the counter, she ordered two chicken empanadas. The solid Mexican in a t-shirt too small for the amount of bosom she possessed, surveyed Linda with caution, immediately fixating on the bruises. Linda felt this same sort of judgment inside the immigration offices. To her, just a bunch of strangers assigning their own endings to a story they never read. Being so close to the U.S. border, the woman spoke a serviceable English answer to Linda's most pressing question, "Do you know where I can make an international call?"

The woman shook her head. "You can buy one of deeze." Reaching under the counter she produced a small flip phone and proceeded to explain the pre-paid plans for tourists as well as the eighteen-dollar automatic refill special – if she wanted it. Linda drank her coffee and ate donuts while the woman entered her information and configured the antiquated gadget. After several signatures on printed pages that she couldn't understand and three failed test calls, the device came to life with an optimistic squawk. Linda fed the remnants of her empanada to the dog on her way by. She collected herself on the passenger's seat and dialed a number.

"Buckshot – Alisha speaking."

"Lish, it's Linda."

"Holy shit, Linda." Alisha whispered. "Where *are*

you?"

"I can't say. Obviously – I'm not coming in today. But, I'm not gonna be in tomorrow either, or – ever. Lish – I need to know – what you know. What the sheriff said. I know he's been and gone by now."

"Randy's gonna freak right the fuck out when I tell him you quit."

A long silence followed. Linda heard clinking plates and muffled voices in the background. "Okay – I didn't talk to Wayne, but Amber said he asked if she talked to you and then sump'n about Joe being hurt real bad."

The news of Joe's continued existence knocked the edge off Linda's biggest fear. She ended the call telling Alisha to take care of herself and just like that, things took on a new light as they're wont to do when one finds out they're no longer running (from the law, anyway). That relief quickly dissolved as she accelerated through the gears, riding the slipstream of an abrupt realization that she had nowhere to go and all day to get there.

Offering up Ensenada to the border agent was a smokescreen. She'd never been before and knew nothing about the place. Operating only on the information put forth by the half-page ad on page six of the atlas touting Hussong's as the birthplace of the margarita, punctuated with glossy photos of scantily-clad caucasians grinding against one another, Linda decided to pass. She opted instead for the small town whose description was relegated to a single sentence on the next page.

With the big city and gringas borrachas off her rear

bumper, the afternoon sun began its descent into the Pacific and encouraged Linda to attempt a descent of her own. Speeding through an atmosphere of fallout and consequences, she felt the highway's convection seep up through her body as a cobalt ocean disappeared to the west. The double-lane asphalt wound its way through valleys and dry vernal pools where the mesquite and cardón stood sentry over spineflower, goldfields, and sage. The Baja wind blasting through the cab tousled Linda's hair and soothed the discolorations in her face. Coffee-colored mountains higher than she imagined rose on both sides. The hills, strewn with granite boulders the size of houses, tinged with pink and mustard hues, kept safe all the world's sorrows.

Steering with a knee, Linda bent the atlas back on itself to the page she needed. Passing through the small pueblos of Los Malcriados and La Grulla alerted her to the approaching turnoff for Santo Tomás. The mission town garnering a smattering of attention in the atlas gave Linda a particle of hope that some sort of marker would alert her to the turn and she was not disappointed to see the bent post supported by a pyramid of river stones. A weathered slat of mesquite, adorned with a crude drawing of what looked to be a crude castle and the words 'Santo Tomás' directed Linda to turn left into an arroyo paralleling the highway.

She downshifted, gouging the trailer hitch into the tarmac as she bounced down a berm onto the impoverished, rutted road. The wheel jerked from side to side and a fine, silky layer of pulverized earth attached itself to everything. She came to a full stop after spooking a drove of donkey grazing at the road's edges. A solitary jack busied himself in the distance.

A short way ahead, Linda coaxed the truck through a water crossing, keeping a steady speed just as her father taught her to do in New Mexico the first time she had to cross the stream that ran full-freshet after the spring rains. "Just keep your speed up, baby," he'd say. "Don't go so fast you shoot a wave or so slow you stall it out."

Clawing her way up a slight embankment on the other side, she glanced in the rearview at muddy tracks and the river behind her. She kept her gaze rearward for too long and missed noticing the large boulder marking the steep-ledged crater she was supposed to avoid. The passenger side of the Tacoma went airborne and landed with a metallic thud. Linda's upper body smashed into the steering wheel. She jammed the truck into reverse and spun a vicious hole with the rear tire. There was a great ruckus and a heavy scent of smoldering rubber, but nothing moved.

"Goddamn it!" Linda skidded herself across the seat and exited on the passenger side. Against the arid backdrop, the truck looked like a wounded soldier on one knee. The front wheel didn't look right, angled like that, tucked high into the fender, higher than it should be. The tears began and right there in the dirt of the arroyo, awash in the fragrance of sweet desert lilac, Linda broke. She allowed it to happen. She wanted it over with. There never was nor would there ever be a better place for a woman to break open – to show her insides to the vultures and the coyote, allow the devils and angels who spilled themselves out prior to enter her – right there in that ditch.

She cried about the fight with Joe – all of the fights. She cried about not being enough to keep him from stepping into the role his father abandoned when he drank himself to death. A role Joe swore he never wanted to play. She cried for the woman she wanted to be, but seemed to have lost. And that made the crying worse. Sobbing so heavily, she thought she might drown; and that someday in the future, someone'd come looking and find her bleached out bones picked clean by scavengers. It was at that moment she felt the need to reel herself in and again think about practical things.

She went for her backpack, throwing it on the hood, she took inventory. As she told the border agent, she had everything she needed. It had been packed that way for the last two years and never became unpacked. It was something Linda did – in the event something happened – as it had the day before. A day when she'd decide to leave – permanently.

In the main compartment, a rain jacket, change of clothes, sleeping bag, 2 pairs of socks, a roll of toilet paper, and an unopened 3-pack of Hanes underwear. A flowery zippered pouch contained a toothbrush and toothpaste, baby wipes, chapstick, tampons, a nail file, and Q-tips. In the outside pocket she kept black and white photocopies of her passport, driver's license, bank cards, and documents related to the truck. A tattered ziplock contained a spare set of truck and house keys, and five one-hundred-dollar bills stuffed tightly into a plastic film canister. Linda finished making sure it was all there, all the while wondering what a psychologist or someone of that nature might say about the woman who keeps a bag packed. In the distance, a small cloud of dust approached. The toy-sized Japanese 4x4 was so rusted through, its body jiggled on its frame.

"Hola, señora!" said the young Mexican with cinnamon skin and a dusting of young adulthood shadowing his upper lip. "Todo bien? He asked with a concerned grin. "Necesita ayuda?"

"If that means do I need help, then the answer is yes... I need help."

Linda apologized for not speaking Spanish. The clear-eyed boy told Linda he understood and that not many gringos out that way did. They were only there to see a three-hundred-year-old mission, and most turned back at the river. He wore a Florida Marlins cap which he spun backwards before diving under the front bumper of Linda's truck. Only a few seconds passed before he emerged shaking his head, swiping his hands together.

"No good," he said, spinning the cap around. "De axle... you know dis? It is broken." He made a gesture with both hands and alternated between Spanish and English words to get his points across. "A dónde va? Where you go?"

"Santo Tomás." Linda said. "I wanted to see the mission, like everyone else."

"I take you," he said opening the passenger door. "I take you to my family's house. I no hurt you. I am

Guillermo. My father, he have tractor. We come – bring you truck." He smiled and wiped dirt from a tattered front seat. "Safe!" He said and then repeated, "Muy seguro."

Linda looked off and wondered – since she hadn't drowned from her tears in the arroyo – if she instead would be done in by a strange Mexican kid in the middle of a desert. "Let me get my pack."

The ten-kilometer ride to Guillermo's ranch in Santo Tomás lasted close to forty-five minutes. Barbed wire stapled to rough-cut lumber encircled a modest ranchito alive with all sorts of animal activity. Dogs were first to greet them, barking, spinning anxious circles and dappling Linda's thighs with dusty paw prints. The goats gathered at a gate. Several chickens, roosters, two small burros, and a half-dozen turkey scattered in different directions startling a sunbaked mule half shaded by a century-old mesquite tree. The frayed hemp rope, shortened by numerous turns around a stake, wrinkled his neck as he lipped scrub from the dirt. A well-worn circle spoke to his accomplishments.

An elderly couple emerged from a windowless home and introduced themselves to Linda as Guillermo Senior and Rosario, the young chauffeur's parents. The son stood smiling with his hands folded behind his back. He spoke rapid words to his father who would, every so often, acknowledge Linda with nods and then turn back to his son for more of the story.

"He tells me your truck is broken just past the river." Guillermo Senior's English was good. Linda's eyes widened with surprise. "You missed the warning, the rock."

"I did. I broke it, good. Your son said you can tow it... with your tractor?"

Senior glanced at the boy, adjusted his straw hat, and said something in Spanish. From what Linda could tell, he was less than happy. Between the diesel fuel he'd burn, plus the wear and tear on his equipment, the chances of him coming out on the losing end of this scenario were high.

Linda broke into the awkwardness saying, "I can pay you. I don't have much and... none of it's in pesos. But..."

Rosario interrupted with something softly over the old man's shoulder. Then she motioned for Linda to follow her saying, "Vamos, chica."

Some moments passed and the churning diesel carrying two Guillermos faded from view. The women smiled at each other from opposite sides of a lopsided barnwood table. Linda wanted to apologize for her imposition. Rosario wanted to know what the American woman with a bruised face was doing in the desert by herself. Rosario went to chopping potatoes. Linda walked to the window where she watched the old mule watching her.

She awoke to the sound of a clicking door, on a dusty sofa, warm beneath a woven blanket. Linda had no memory of falling asleep. The Guillermos stomped the desert from their boots and walked to a sink in another room to wash up. Across the room, under the harsh light of bare bulbs, Rosario began assembling supper plates with slabs of meat, roasted potatoes and carrots. Linda tried to gather up how many hours she'd been out and rushed to help. The weary men came to the table one behind the other. Junior spoke first. "It's here. Your truck is safe."

"You know – y'all might get a few more visitors with a better road."

"Bad roads bring good people," said Senior. "Good roads bring everyone else."

Linda didn't know what to say next. She put plates on the table, folded napkins, and avoided obvious questions. Senior said, "I will start in the morning. We'll know then." His thick, black hair stood-up high, damp and disheveled. A hat-band indentation ran from one gray temple to the other. There were no more words, only the gentle clicking of knives and forks on brittle ceramic. At times during the meal, Linda looked up to see Junior smiling at her, and from across the table, Rosario's exacting, suspicious glances.

***

The rooster's uneven ruckus woke Linda before dawn; her body ached from a restless night. Wiping sleep from her eyes, she stepped out into the chill of a desert morning. Greeted with soft snorts, Linda untangled the old mule's tether from the stake, loosened the lasso around his neck, and massaged the hairless patch. The mule issued confidential rumbles of approval.

Linda needed to pee. Already feeling like an invader, asking to use the family's bathroom raised her anxiety. Without rousting the chickens, she stepped around back of the unstable coop, undid the button on her jeans, and leaned her bare backside against the chilly corrugated tin. With a large amount of uncertainty of how the day would play out, she started back to the house. Seeing a pair of legs jutting from beneath her truck startled her. She squatted to see it was Senior.

"Good morning," her voice cracked.

"You don't have to pee outside. We are not animals," he said pulling hard on a wrench.

"I'm sorry," she said, with a bit of embarrassment. "I didn't want... I've put you to a lot of trouble already, I didn't want to ask for anything else."

With both hands, Guillermo slid his body out and sat up, face to face with Linda. "It cannot be fixed today... and not tomorrow. I don't know how long to get parts. They must come from Tijuana. Maybe a week... possibly two. I can't say the cost." He ran fingers through his hair. "It's no good to begin the day this way. Let's go – Rosario will make breakfast."

Inside, the smell of beef and onions announced the day. Rosario patted balls of maize and lard into paper-thin tortillas and laid them to cook on a mesquite-fired comal. Linda joined the Guillermos at the table. Coffee was poured. From a saucer, Junior stirred in teaspoons of heated goat milk. Linda did the same. Rosario arrived with a platter containing the remnants of beef from the previous night's dinner, a small mound of huevos revueltos, four sausage links, and a puddle of refried beans topped with cream and cotija. Steam rose from a covered plate of molten tortillas. Rosario placed a napkin in her lap and folded her hands under her chin. "Buen provecho."

Linda feared another wordless meal fraught with silent judgments. Addressing senior directly as the only one able to fully understand her words, Linda said, "My husband punched me... in the face."

Senior paused the arrangement of his eggs. Rosario softly cleared her throat and took a two-handed sip from her coffee. Junior ceased all chewing and stared directly at Linda. All of them conveying an understanding via glassy eyes.

"I know y'all are wondering. I didn't mean for it to come out like that... didn't mean to be rude. I know how this looks, me out here alone – unprepared. I don't know where I'm headed, but I'll leave out today. You've been kind to me. You deserve the truth, no matter how uncomfortable it is for me to say. I... wanted to be honest." Linda began eating with birdlike bites. She made direct eye contact with Rosario and offered a slight smile, permission to acknowledge her truth. Tasting the bottom of her coffee cup, she excused herself from the table. Senior met her outside.

"That mule is useless."

"Is he more or less useless than a pickup with a busted axle?"

Senior raised his brow and laughed for the first time. "I learned my English in California. I went with my uncle León. I was eighteen. For two years I live in Crescent City. It was beautiful. This place, you know?"

Linda nodded a confirmation.

"We work the lumber barges before the earthquake. After – there was no more work. There was nothing.

The waves carried it away. I will never forget. In the night, the ocean went away, barges were on the bottom. Then the water rushed back in a wall." Guillermo's eyes lifted to an apparition high above Linda's head. "It was an explosion of cars, buildings, people – all the trees from the lumber yard – the city, everything destroyed. Tanks of gasolina start to blow up. The water rushed out and back, again and again. We watch our docks disappear, timber barges flip like toys. We tried to save things, but – it was too much. My uncle León fell in the water... he could not swim. I try to save him. I could not. So many people. My friends, my family."

"Oh, Guillermo – I'm so sorry."

"That is my honesty."

The sun warmed them. Guillermo said, "My son can take you where you need to go. I will fix your truck when I get parts. You can pay when you return." Linda thought about her answer. Stroking the old mule's nose, she said, "I got a better idea. That old Suzuki of yours is 'bout dead. How 'bout... you keep my truck. I'll take this guy, right here."

Guillermo's boisterous laugh spooked the chickens. "Forgive me, Señora, but you want to trade your truck for a useless mule? What will you do with a Mule?"

"Ride him. You gotta have a saddle 'round here somewhere. I'm gonna see this country the way it's supposed to be seen."

"Child – look at you. What man would I be to let an American woman ride off into the desert on an old mule? Do you know about rattlesnakes and bobcat;

scorpion and coyote? That mule hasn't earned a day's hay since Guillermo was a child. He no want to work. I would be sending you to your death."

"Don't you worry about me. I rode when I was younger. I'll handle my business. I survived nineteen years with an abusive man, bobcat don't scare me."

Linda cinched the girth strap. She hugged the family members one by one, then mounted the confused animal. The two Guillermos and Rosario appeared confused as well, unsure of what to make of the American woman atop a mule, wearing a colorful backpack and impractical shoes. Junior, however, wore an expression that suggested otherwise. The young man was witnessing an angel sprout wings and take flight. To Rosario's dismay, a portion of the boy's heart was flying off with her.

Linda smiled broadly and said, "Thanks for everything. God bless y'all." She tugged the reigns lightly to the side and spun the mule south. Within seconds of wandering, he was farther away from that stake in the ground than he'd been years. Senior felt a great responsibility for letting the woman ride off. Fearing eternal judgment from his creator, he trotted after the unlikely pair with Junior on his heels. "Señora! Señora! Please, I fear for your safety!" said the seventy-four-year-old Guillermo with heavy breaths. "What will I tell those who come looking for you, your husband?"

"My husband... ain't looking for me, I promise. Nobody's coming for me."

"Señora, please... they will come and they will ask. What will I tell them? That I let you ride into the desert alone? They will call me a fool and throw me in jail. Señora..."

Linda and the two Guillermos traded expressions. She was sympathetic to Senior's concern. Having to explain away a gringa's disappearance while in full possession of her vehicle could present some difficulty for the man.

"Guillermo," she said. "Nobody's gonna come lookin' for me. And I promise I'll come by on my way back. You'll see. Me and this old mule are gonna be just fine together."

Junior interrupted the moment, "Señora... why? Why you come here, to Santo Tomás?"

"I don't know, Guillermo. It just seemed like as good a place as any to meet a stranger."

Dominoes

To make himself nervous, he'd stand with his toes cantilever over the yellow line like one of those Acapulco cliff divers, the buzzing of the perilous third rail harmonizing with that of his own familiar zizz. He'd wait until the preemptive cushion of underground air announcing the train breathed warm in his face before he'd retreat to stand with the other sheep returning home to unfulfilled lives after a day of unfulfilling work.

Shuffling his way through the throng of commuters with closed fists drawn up into his jacket sleeves, he tried to touch nothing. Rubbing shoulders with strangers or feeling a man's dense crotch pressing against his backside sent him streaking for the remotest corners of the rail car. This debilitating uneasiness and clinical level of introversion he attributed directly to his *fucking parents*, a term of endearment he insisted on when referring to them in therapy sessions, which took place on regular Wednesdays and also required him to ride a train. *"You have to be a special kinda asshole to shingle a kid with a name that virtually guarantees he'll be crammed through a keyhole of abuse for the rest of his godforsaken life. Either they were trying to build character or... raise an axe murderer."* Those were his words.

The truth of the matter was, aside from transporting himself between his furniture-less apartment and his passionless place of employment, voluntary outings were kept to a minimum or avoided altogether. If a need arose to venture outside (and one rarely did), it almost always coincided with a desire for take-out from Titt's, a small brewpub that sat catty-corner on Durham Street at Germantown Avenue, just a few hundred yards from his front door. His order never varied: Bavarian pretzel with whole grain mustard. Brussels sprouts with toasted pumpkin seeds, cranberries, Grana Padano cheese, and a side of orange thyme vinaigrette. A twelve-inch Continental flatbread pizza with garlic puree, bacon, fig, asiago cheese, and arugula. And a growler of Bazoombas Porter. None of which the twenty-nine-year-old Wishful Means ever finished, but instead, dwelled in the high hopes and possibility that one day he might. He was a man of calculated seclusion who traveled an immutable light rail of existence. That's precisely what made his accepting the invitation to a social gathering being thrown by co-workers so surprising.

Approaching the rear of the train car and running

out of options for corners to back himself into, Wish spotted a conspicuously vacant seat next to a conspicuously attractive woman. Immediately, his mind ripped through a litany of imagined complaints: foul-smelling body odor, chronic halitosis, Tourette's, stinky feet... flatulence. What a shame for a woman with such perfect eyebrows. Quickly, the awkward moment arrived when he found himself adjacent to her seat and had to decide to sit or pass it by. Passengers brushed against him, while others stared, and it seemed to Wish as though several had a considerable investment in his decision. This sent an inferno through him, triggering an act of intrepid boldness; he sat down next to the lady with the eyebrows. Their thighs touched. She shifted.

She was young looking, Lebanese, he imagined, and neither buxom nor noticeably frail, with a head of silky hair the color of ebony. Her pantsuit appeared to be made of a natural fabric, light ash in color, and sufficiently professional, and he detected no immediate off-putting odors. She wasn't mumbling to herself or to others, and therefore, any evaluation as to the conditions inside her mouth was impossible. The tips of her shoes appeared fresh and unscuffed. He couldn't possibly recognize their maker, but imagined a designer's name embossed in gold, running the full length of her arch.

He didn't dare turn his head and look at her directly for any of this indexing – although the fervid desire to glimpse at her brows from an up-close vantage point was oppressive. Instead, Wish strained the muscles of his eyes downward, as he did in the seventh grade when he ogled Kelley Grey's bare knees. Tracing his gaze from the woman's shoe tips, he admired her manicured hands resting gently in her lap, but quickly shifted focus to the severed finger bobbing in an opaque plastic cup half-filled with a clear liquid, waiting to take root. There was no longer any gray area regarding the open seat next to an attractive woman on a packed train.

Wish covered his mouth with two sleeved fists and began coughing uncontrollably. Several swaying passengers offered pitying grins when he met their stares. His face flushed with heat. He was drawing unwanted attention. The woman turned and met his eyes directly with no change to her face or the slightest hint at an explanation. Finally, Wish could properly survey her magnificent eyebrows. (Though he thought better of touching them without an invitation, considering the plastic cup and all). After a significant amount of uncomfortableness she said, "Maybe you should just mind your own business."

To which he replied, quietly, and with a slight nod, "That seems like a very reasonable request."

When the doors allowed it, Wish evacuated the train. Moving at a slow jog across the congested platform and up piss-damp steps, he broke the surface onto 11th Street and gasped a chestful of fresher air. Questioning his decision to interact with the public and dreading the about-face required for another train ride home, Wish carried on by foot the last nine or so blocks through the streets of Fishtown, eventually arriving at the Chesterman Building on Memphis

Street, where he stood for a solid ten minutes, vacillating between pushing the buzzer and not pushing the buzzer. He delayed the decision further by strolling to a shed-sized coffee trailer across the way and, after some dithering, settled on an overly complex chai latte before returning to push the button.

Following a brief conversation with a metallic speaker, Wish climbed the stairs with a somber procedural march, stalling at each landing. From the flight above, a woman composed of ancient features descended with the pace of a glacier. Remembering his manners, Wish rushed to greet the woman mid-flight and attempted to brace her.

"Please," he said, "let me help."

She met his gesture of samaritanism with an abrupt elbow to the chest. "Getcher fuckin' hands off-a me!"

Wish stumbled, recovered briefly, then tripped over his feet and landed hard on his backside, fully dowsed in warm latte. "Lovely – chivalry's dead, alright – and now we know who killed it," said Wish from his knees. "... dead as a fucking doornail." The woman continued her descent, scuffing the walls, never acknowledging he'd said a word. From atop the last flight, Wish shouted over the banister, "Have a wonderful night, now... Cruella!"

The door to apartment 3A swung open. Zoe Matthews, its occupant, puzzled at the sight of Wish straining himself over the railing said, "Wish? What the hell's going on?"

"Oh, just berating octogenarians."

"What happened?"

"Creepy old lady punched me – spilled my chai. Fucked up my chi a little, too."

"Mrs. DeLeo? Oh, shit... you didn't try to touch her did you?"

"I *tried* to help her down the stairs. The woman's older than God... and meaner."

"You got off easy. She kicked the UPS guy in the nuts."

Brushing past Zoe in the doorway, Wish let her scent of lemongrass tinged with sweet bonfire smoke displace the baked garbage aroma he'd been carrying in his nose since the subway. Running his eyes over the surfaces in her one-bedroom apartment, it struck him that it looked nothing like he'd imagined. This was because Wish never actually imagined he'd ever be standing in Zoe's apartment at all. Admiring her choices of light grays, chocolate browns, and splashes of lavender, he ran an uninvited finger along an alphabetized bookshelf and gathered up a framed photo of Zoe and a man.

"Take your clothes off."

"What?" Wish spun to see Zoe holding a lustrous floral robe. His face rushed red.

"Go in the bathroom and put this on. I'll run down to the laundry room and wash your clothes. You're not going to the party like that."

"Oh – God no. I'm not going to the party. I'm just gonna... head home." With that, Wish made for the door. "This night's been a total disaster."

Zoe protested, trailing closely. "C'mon, Wish. You're here... the party doesn't start for another hour at least. Don't leave."

Wish let himself out and descended the stairs with a slight gallop, all the while disassembling, then reassembling the thought process that's kept him rocketing through the contemptible reality of his life. He wanted more than anything to overthrow the usual suspects rioting within him, the ones that left him lying on his living room floor in the dark, bound and gagged in his own perceived flaws.

Wish paused at the ground floor, seeing that just beyond the double-glass door, the four-foot-tall badger known as Mrs. DeLeo, was scanning the block for small children to eat. Not wanting to risk an attack on his vulnerable balls, he tucked himself neatly into a corner next to the mailbox slots and – calming himself with deep breaths – was soon elsewhere, transported to a magicless childhood and the first realization that his life would be spattered with conflict: the fifth-grade fistfight with Tommy Arbuckle after Tommy replaced the masking tape name-badge on Wish's locker with *Pissful Streams*. More reprimands followed, along with parent conferences, suspensions, and more nicknames; none of them very creative, all of them sufficiently damaging. Within the confines of the stairwell and with only a few bundles of orphaned mail as witnesses, Wish arrived at the notion that if things were to look different moving forward – if the victimization of Wishful Means was to cease – the first domino needed to fall immediately.

"Excuse me, Mrs. DeLeo?" he said, tapping furiously on the woman's skeletal collar bone, fearing his finger might poke through. "The next time someone attempts to help you down the stairs, a simple no thank you will suffice."

As expected, the little badger went for his balls. Armed with Zoe's intel, Wish was ready with a stutter-step maneuver that resembled some sort of skipping motion mixed with a few of the uncomfortable elements in the electric slide. Either way, she missed him completely, yet her actions were not entirely without results. As it happened, the small woman threw so much action into the acceleration of her leg, she knocked herself off balance. Wish saw her teeter-totter happening in slow-motion, but was unable to react quickly enough. The old woman staggered and began to topple. To her great misfortune, the SEPTA bus scheduled to arrive at that exact spot at that exact moment was surprisingly punctual and caused Mrs. DeLeo to become flat as a gum wrapper.

Wish rapped lightly on Zoe's door, clinging to the very last of the high hopes he'd begun the evening with.

"Wish – you're still here? I was about to run down and see what the sirens..."

"Mrs. DeLeo got hit by a bus."

Zoe smiled and spoke through a slight chuckle. "That's not funny."

"I'm being serious. She tried to kick me in nuts. She missed and tripped off the curb. The 7:05 squashed'er like a bug."

"Holy shit!"

"She's in a better place. Who knew you could get there by bus."

Zoe gazed at Wish, her mouth open in disbelief. He

wanted to kiss her. Instead, he said, "Can we start over? I don't want to go home."

"Okay, sure."

"Did I tell you that I sat next to a woman with a severed finger? She had the most magnificent eyebrows I've ever seen."

"That's how you start over?"

"You don't think that's a significant development?"

"You wanna come in?"

"Do we have to go to the party?"

"Not if you don't want to."

"Then yes."

Brushing past her in the doorway for the second time, Wish allowed the flood of Zoe to wash away the dominoes.

What would it look like
if you followed the light inside
and refused to listen
to the voices telling you no?

About the Author

 Chris DiCroce is an author, songwriter, and — a quitter.

He quit the rat-race, sold his Nashville home, and nearly everything he owned and moved aboard a small sailboat, in search of a simpler life. Since that time, he's authored several Amazon bestselling books, numerous magazine pieces, and sailed to eight countries.

DiCroce's been writing in one form or another for over 30 years. As a young songwriter and artist in Nashville, Tennessee, he wrote and produced three critically-acclaimed records. His music and introspective lyrics captured the attention of the New York Times and the industry's top publications such as Billboard Magazine and Performing Songwriter.

He toured nationally and internationally, performing at FARM AID, for the USO, and as the support act for numerous artists including Robert Plant, Steve Forbert, and the Samples.

In 2001, a divorce and the events of September 11th

forced DiCroce to reexamine everything, setting in motion a journey of reinvention that ultimately led to his leaving Nashville in 2012.

DiCroce began experimenting and writing in long-form. His pieces on travel and minimalist living have been featured in SAIL Magazine and SpinSheet Magazine, and he's been featured on numerous podcasts including iHeart Radio's Speaking of Travel, Boat Radio International, and the Tiny House Lifestyle Podcast.

A staunch minimalist, DiCroce quietly champions the virtues of a simpler life through speaking engagements.

He's currently working on his next project from his favorite taqueria in Mexico where he lives part-time with his wife Melody.

To find out more, visit chrisdicroce.com.

Other Books by Chris DiCroce

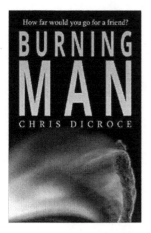

Burning Man

How far would you go for a friend?

One week ago, music legend Dash Nelson was on the way down. His music, iconic. Revered. And, it's not selling. But he's got one more record in him and it just might be his best one yet.

On the morning after the record release party for Heavy Clutch, Dash is roused from a scotch-induced slumber with the news that his long-time manager and best friend, Paul West, was found dead.

Dash abandons his family, friends, and his record to keep a promise he made to Westie many years ago. A promise that pushes Dash to the limits of his own sanity. A promise that he's certain will land him in prison, and leaves him fighting for his life aboard a sailboat with Westie's biggest secret.

From Dash and Westie's aeonic friendship comes BURNING MAN. A simmering novel that twists in the grasp of DiCroce's unique storytelling.

You Gotta Go To Know

"Every minute you spend wishing you did something is a minute you spend not doing it."

Tired of the status quo, Chris and Melody, along with their Dutch Shepherd, Jet, sold their Nashville home and almost everything they owned to move onto a 35-foot sailboat and go cruising.

This is the story of a leap of faith - from making the decision, finding the right boat, downsizing and selling everything, and finally telling friends, family, and bosses.

Once on board, they discovered that their greatest triumphs often came from their greatest challenges. Champagne wishes and caviar dreams soon fell prey to their bologna sandwich and Miller High Life budget. Boat breakdowns, tropical storms, and over-extended bank accounts brought them face-to-face with the reality that things don't always go as planned. But sometimes... that's the best plan.

Light-hearted, humorous, and sometimes sad, this story will draw you in you with its unique look at life on a sailboat and the emotions that come with it.

If you've ever wanted to sell it all, buy a boat, and sail away, this is a book you'll want to read.

What's Up Ditch!

If you're thinking about doing a boat trip down the Atlantic Intracoastal Waterway, this is a book to add to your arsenal of information.

What's Up Ditch is a personal perspective based on observations and the navigation logs of Chris DiCroce, an avid sailor who has traveled the ICW on his sailboat six times. He walks you through many of the situations you might encounter along the waterway, and includes protocols and ideas on everything from hailing a bridge to maximizing a budget over the course of this 1000 + mile trip. He discusses how much boat you really need, how to figure out fuel usage, VHF radio protocol, tides, currents, and more.

What's Up Ditch! is not a "waterway guide." It's not meant to take the place of, but rather complement, the many great resources available to boaters today.

The ICW is "back-alley America at six miles an hour" and can take sixteen days or sixteen weeks. It's a trip full of challenges and learning opportunities, and this book addresses a lot of what you'll need to know. From the Dismal Swamp to the Virginia Cut, you'll get a viewpoint you may not have read in the past. The Atlantic ICW will test your navigation skills, boat-handling skills, and your patience, but in the end, it will reward you with gorgeous scenery and an experience you'll not soon forget.

If you've ever thought about doing the ICW, or even if you've done some or all of it, there's something here for you. It's a no-nonsense approach with Chris' usual bad jokes and some well-placed sarcasm. Beware you magenta line hugging boaters... there's something in there about you as well!

What's Up Ditch! will challenge you and encourage you. It will break down and dissect some of the issues that might be keeping you from doing one of the coolest trips we have right here in America.

Acknowledgement

To Melody: thank you for your tireless dedication and unwavering support. Here's to the stories we've written together and to those yet to come.